SECOND WIND

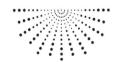

CEILLIE SIMKISS

CONTENT WARNINGS

THE DOG DOES NOT DIE AND THERE IS NO ACTUAL DEATH IN THIS NOVELLA.

- Mention of spousal death,
- spreading of ashes,
- discussion of service dog duties and types of seizures,
- mentions of chronic pain and illness,
- mentions of ageism,
- mentions of pregnancy in family member.

There is also a nonbinary child who uses she/her pronouns. This is not a mistake.

For any questions about content, feel free to email me at contact@candidceillie.com or DM me on Twitter at @CandidCeillie.

CHAPTER ONE

MARTHA - 1955

I KNOCKED AS HARD AS I COULD ON THE FRONT DOOR OF the little yellow farmhouse, bouncing on my toes while I waited for someone to answer .

Less than a minute later, Margaret Thornton opened the door. She was already fully dressed, with her face on and her hair curled, despite the fact that the sun was just barely peeking over the treeline. I'd run down in just my pajamas.

"Hello Martha. You're here early. Pamela isn't up yet." She pursed her lips at me in a way that said she wasn't really surprised.

"Ms. Peggy, I came to ask you a question. Can Pammy come out with me today?" My words tumbled out in an excitable rush. "Mama and Daddy are taking us to the river for a swim and a picnic but it won't be any fun if it's just me 'n David."

The air on the covered porch was so hot and wet, I

1

might as well have been swimming in the river already. I wished I was.

"Pleeeeeeease, Ms. Peggy?"

She broke into a smile and opened the door wide enough for me to pass through.

"Sure. But you get to wake her up. Have you eaten yet?"

"No, ma'am! Daddy's already prepping food for the picnic and said we could wait to eat till we'd worked up a real appetite."

Her tinkling laugh filled the hallway as I skipped to Pammy's room down the hall.

"I'll call your mother and tell her I'm making you pancakes, then. Maybe she'll join us for breakfast."

MARTHA

"Mom, are you sure you don't want me to go with you? I can buy a ticket and join you."

Concern was written all over the fine lines on my daughter's face. I smiled wryly at my daughter from underneath the round magenta sunglasses I wore.

"What, do you think I can't handle a week on my own?"

Andrea licked her lips and blew her blonde bangs out of her eyes before she answered. A couple of people shot us dirty looks as we stood just outside of the security line. I assumed we were in the way.

"It's not that I don't think you can handle it, exactly," she hedged. "It's just the first time you've traveled alone and you're flying out of the country to spread Dad's ashes.

It's a lot, and I want you to know that you don't have to do it all by yourself."

Her worry was touching. It was true that I hadn't traveled on my own before. When I'd been young and unmarried, it hadn't been appropriate for a girl to travel without her chaperone, but Joseph and I had made this journey nearly a dozen times over the 42 years we'd been married. It was as familiar a path as the one that took me to the home I'd grown up in. I took her hand in my much more wrinkled one and squeezed, putting all of my love into the touch.

"Travelling on my own can't be any harder than traveling with two kids, or with you and the grandkids, Andy. Your father and I made this plan before you and your brother were even thought of, and I intend to see it through."

I was proud that my voice never trembled, even if she wouldn't have been able to hear that over the crush of voices and beeping of the security officer's wands.

The truth was, the idea of taking this journey with my husband's ashes instead of with his living, breathing self was breaking my heart, but I wouldn't let that show. Not now. It would be exactly what she needed to buy her own ticket and come with me, despite the financial hardship it would put her in.

"I need to take this last trip, Andrea. We'll figure out everything else when I get back, but for now... I need to do this. For your father and for myself."

My daughter was watching my face. I knew she was looking for any sign of me second guessing my decision, but she wouldn't find it. He'd been gone for more than a year now, and it was time for me to do what I'd promised him I would. She laid her hand atop mine and we stood there in silence for a moment before I spoke again with forced cheer in my voice.

"Now, it's time for me to get in line, dear. But I will call you the instant I'm out of the airport."

"Promise?" In that moment, she sounded just like she had the first time her father and I had travelled without her and her brother at the age of seven. I beamed at her and squeezed her hand.

"I promise."

Half an hour later, I'd made it through the line and said goodbye to my daughter. TSA had found nothing interesting in my baggage, aside from Joseph's ashes, but since I had declared them and had all the required paperwork, they'd waved me through.

I still couldn't believe the airline had required me to purchase him his own seat. It wasn't like I was traveling with his casket. He was packaged in a hermetically sealed bag, then tucked into a box the size of a sheaf of printer paper. But I wasn't going to make a fuss over it. I had the money, courtesy of his life insurance policy. It would at least make sure I had some extra space to move around in while we flew.

The flight from Philadelphia to Glasgow was nearly 12 hours long, and even at the ripe age of 70, there was no way I could sleep for that long. One could only hope that the people I'd be seated with would be interesting.

PAMELA

Crouton was nervous. She kept twitching her ears and whining at every creak and roar the bus made as it made its way from the long term parking to the airport. I was glad we were the only ones on the bus because clearly, we had not done enough training on public transportation for her to be comfortable. I made a note in my phone to tell her soon-to-be handler.

The rest of the seven month old poodle's training seemed to hold once we entered the airport. She stayed by my side while we stood in line without a worry, keeping an eye out for anything concerning, but not chasing anything or anyone - even when we came across another corgi. She had taken to her work as a service dog well, and I was glad for it.

She had been one of only two from her litter of five who'd had the temperament and attention span they'd needed to be a service dog, which was a big change for me. My nephew had made me promise to slow down a little bit, and that was certainly one way to make sure I did it.

"71 year old women shouldn't be spending every hour of every day with dogs that go on to serve other people," he'd told me. "You should be enjoying your silver years with a dog that's going to be there for you if you don't want a partner."

It was sweet, really, even if it was ridiculous. He and I had always gotten along quite well. If he had his way, I'd have been living with him and his husband years ago. Except his husband was allergic to dogs, which would cramp my style on so many levels. It wasn't a perfect solution, but I appreciated the sentiment.

Maybe it would be something we could discuss further once I returned home from Glasgow.

"Oh, she's beautiful," the TSA agent crooned. "Such a lovely brown girl. I'd pet her if she wasn't working."

I smiled at him while he inspected the paperwork. Crouton's official color was apricot, which only someone ensconced in the dog world would know.

"I appreciate the restraint. Most people don't seem to even notice the vest, even though it's bright orange."

"Some people just have no manners," he said mournfully. "What's her name?"

"Crouton!"

He laughed out loud, a deep booming laugh that made me and several people around him smile, too.

"Well, Ms. Thornton, I hope you and Crouton have a lovely flight. Whoever sits next to you is a lucky human."

With a grin that I hoped would have charmed all the young ladies when I was their age, I swept through the rest of the line and we made our way to the terminal where our flight would be boarding in little more than an hour.

MARTHA

There was a sort of peace that always came with boarding a flight for me. Standing in line with other people, checking your board passes at the gate. When Joseph had been with me, I would have spent the time holding back giggles at the stories he came up with for the people in line with us. People-watching and crafting stories about them had been one of our favorite traveling pastimes.

It was almost disconcerting now to not have his rough baritone murmuring in my ear, telling me the story of the woman in footie pajamas or the man talking animatedly about bees on a bluetooth headset. But when I saw a slim woman who looked to be about my age with a shock of fiery red hair that almost matched her sweater and a beautiful warm brown standard poodle in a service vest, the only voice in my head was my own.

My God, she's stunning.

I couldn't deny what my brain was saying. I wasn't sure what it was about her that drew my eye. It could have been the kind smile on her face as she spoke to a young man on the other side of her or the sparkle in her bright blue eyes when she glanced in my direction. I couldn't take my eyes off of her until those eyes focused on me. Then I couldn't look away fast enough as she was called ahead of most of the line to board the plane.

Something about the way she held herself was familiar, but I couldn't quite place what it was. I shook my head, sure that I was imagining a connection with her just because she was attractive. I knew there was no way that I could have forgotten someone as captivating as she was, even at my age.

Slowly but surely the line moved forward and I passed through the gate to board the airplane that would take me on the last flight I intended to take to Glasgow.

All I had to do now was get to my seat and make sure that Joseph was safely situated. I took a deep breath and walked to my designated seats, only to find that someone was already seated in the end seat of my row as well as one of the seats that was supposed to be mine.

Not just someone. The woman I'd been admiring in line and her service dog. She looked up at me, confusion adding new lines to her age-wrinkled forehead.

"Can I help you?" Her voice sounded like molten silver, deep but clear and joyful. I almost forgot that I was supposed to respond. Almost. I cleared my throat.

"I think you're in my seat?"

Her eyebrows jumped to her hairline, and the feeling that I knew her returned with a surge.

"I most certainly am not!" She thrust two tickets at my face, nearly poking the lenses of my glasses. "See for yourself!"

I took the tickets from her and blinked several times at what I saw there. My mouth went dry.

"Pamela Thornton? Your name is Pamela Thornton?"

"Yes? Is that a problem?" She was looking at me like she thought I was losing my mind. Honestly, I thought I might be, too, judging by the way my heart was racing and how hard I was clutching her tickets.

"Did you live in Blairsville in the 50's?" My voice was breathy. Her face scrunched in what looked like a mix confusion and concern.

"Yes, I did. Is that a problem?"

I hadn't been imagining her familiarity. For the first twelve years of my life, I had known this woman better than I'd known myself.

"Pammy?" My voice was barely a whisper. "I didn't think I'd ever see you again. It's me, Martha."

CHAPTER TWO

MARTHA - 1968

Pam and I had not spoken in over a week. I knew when she'd gotten upset, but I wasn't sure what I'd done to upset her.

All of the other girls in our classes wouldn't stop talking about how they felt about the boys, and I had joined in, talking about how cute I thought Bobby Jones was. Because I did. He had finally started to grow into his gangly limbs to all of the work he did on his dad's farm, and he always had something to say.

Pammy had made a face that reminded me of when she ate sour grapes and refused to talk for the rest of the day without giving me a reason why. It wasn't the first time it happened, either.

I loved her more than anyone else in the world, but I couldn't stand the way she went from treating me like her best friend to treating me like a stranger. So, today, I had a plan. I would be biking to her house and we were going to talk about whatever kept making her so upset, and we were going to figure it out.

We had been friends for thirteen years. She hated conflict, but sometimes there was no avoiding it. I couldn't remember ever peddling faster than I had that day, or afterward. Not even when we raced. Only, when I got to her house, all I could see was a moving truck.

The entire house was empty. Two strange men sat in the cab of the truck, munching on sandwiches that smelled like they had been left in the heat for too long.

"You lost, little girl?" One man asked, his mouth still full. I glared up at him. Who was he to think he belonged here and that I didn't?

"Are you?" I retorted. "Why are you packing up all of the Thornton's stuff? Where are they?"

"They moved to Philly, baby," the other man informed me. "They hired us to come get everything they couldn't fit in their car. You need a ride somewhere?"

I rolled my eyes at him and walked into the house. Walking from room to room, all I saw was hardwood floors and empty walls. It was surreal. To see all of the empty spaces where there should have been furniture and photographs, to hear silence where I should have heard the chatter of the radio and Ryan's delighted laughter as he played with his favorite train set... it was like all the light and joy had gone out of my world and someone had punched me in the gut at the same time.

The entire family was gone. The truck was pulling out of the driveway and any proof that they had ever lived there was going with it. I couldn't believe it.

Pammy hadn't even bothered to tell me she was leaving. How could she not have told me? I couldn't imagine why, or how, she would have kept this a secret from me. Then the reality of the situation hit me. Her parents had been spending every weekend in Philadelphia for the last few months. They'd taken all of their things with them. What were the chances that I would ever actually see her again?

Math may not have been my strong suit, but I knew a lost cause when I saw one. I fell to the floor and let myself break into full body sobs, knowing that my heart had been broken for the very first time.

———

PAMELA - 2019

My heart, and my jaw, dropped into my stomach at the woman's words. I opened my mouth then closed it, then opened it again.

"Martha?" My voice shook on the word that was pinging around my brain as I looked at the woman who had just shaken me to my core. "Martha Rodgers?"

"I, um, it's Appleby now," she laughed softly, swaying slightly where she stood in the aisle with a duffel bag.

Suddenly, a young white woman in a flight attendant's uniform stood beside her in the aisle. Martha jumped when she noticed her. She was shorter and slimmer than Martha, with eyes that were the same color as her brunette ponytail but had enough of a presence to draw both of our eyes.

"Ladies, is there a problem here?"

Martha and I exchanged a glance that somehow felt both entirely familiar and brand new at the same time. Crouton put a paw on my arm, bringing me back to myself.

11

"Um, not really? I think there's been some sort of mix-up with our tickets." My voice was still wobbly. How could it not be? The woman I'd grown up loving with was standing less than two feet away from me, for the first time in more than fifty years. If I was being honest with myself, I was surprised I hadn't fainted when she'd told me her name.

"May I see them?" Her tone was polite, but firm, in a way that said she'd done this thousands of times before.

"Oh!" Martha laughed at herself again. She handed over both of my tickets and... two of her own. Was she traveling with someone? A spouse? Whoever gave her the name Appleby.

A glance at her hands, now empty and clutching each other, told me there were no rings on her hands, but the ring finger on the left one had an indentation that looked like it could have come from a wedding band.

"These do appear to have the same number," the attendant interrupted. "Let me see what I can find out about this."

The attendant tapped the seat numbers into her tablet, frowning. Her face cleared when something on her screen beeped.

"I seem to have found the issue. Apparently, the airline overbooks service animals and seat for remains, since they usually go unused. So technically, you've both paid for the seat in the middle here." She gestured to the seat where Crouton sat, happily watching the exchange. Remains. What did she mean by that? I blinked at her, confused, until it dawned on me.

The indent on her ring finger. The new name. At our age? That added up to one thing.

"However, the seat on either side of the shared seat are

available for each of you to sit in. I'm sorry for the confusion. If there's nothing else I can do for you?" She barely waited before giving us her best customer service smile and walking back down the aisle.

I tried to hide the fact that I couldn't take my eyes off of Martha. Her tall, sturdy frame was wrapped in an elegant gray wool peacoat and a pair of black pants that hugged her muscular legs tightly.

"Well. I guess that's that, then." Martha said, her voice more controlled than mine had been. Her lips still trembled. "Pardon me. I'll have to squeeze past you, and they don't make that easy with how tight these aisles are."

She shoved her duffel bag into the overhead compartment, holding on to the pale pink purse that matched her large, round glasses. That had been her favorite color when we were younger. I was glad to see that at least one thing hadn't changed since the last time I'd seen her. My heart flipped in my chest, and I had to amend that statement. Two things hadn't changed since then.

She took a breath so deep it strained the buttons of her coat and looked at the space she had to get through with trepidation.

"Here, let me get up so you don't have to squeeze past me," I said, standing up as quickly as I could. Except she'd already started her way into the aisle. In a blink, we were colliding. Everything happened so fast that I barely had time to notice that I was falling until I felt her catch me in her arms and Crouton's cold nose nudged my elbow.

My heart thumped unevenly as I stared up at her. Her blue eyes were just as bright as I remembered them, even though her face was much more wrinkled and the curls I remembered as a mousy blonde had faded to a crisp, beautiful white. She was even more beautiful than I'd imagined she would be at this age, and stronger than I'd expected. I'd never wanted to be the damsel in distress in any situation, but damn if it didn't feel good to be held.

Her lips quirked up into a crooked smile and she leaned back, allowing me to pull myself into a position where I could stand on my own.

"I see you haven't gotten any more graceful since I saw you last."

"What can I say? Some things never change." I huffed a laugh, brushing myself off with embarrassment. I knew my cheeks were a similar color to my hair but there was nothing I could do. "Crouton, get back in your seat."

The dog obeyed, as usual, allowing me to step out into the aisle. Martha's smile evened out and she made her way to the window seat that was hers for the duration of the flight. I sat back down in the aisle seat, petting Crouton's head gently. This flight was going to be much more fun than I'd thought.

MARTHA

"Not a good flyer?"

"Hm?" My fingers shook as I clicked my seatbelt into place. Apparently, Pammy had noticed. She gave me a soft smile when I clasped my hands together. "Oh. No, I was just... surprised. I just. I didn't think I'd ever see you again."

Her smile tightened.

"Neither did I, but apparently the universe had other plans for us."

"Yeah, well, the universe could have stepped in earlier, don't you think?"

She laughed, and it was like no time had passed at all. It was still closer to a witch's cackle than the delicate laugh her mother had wanted for her only daughter, with just a hint of gravel at the bottom of her voice. Hearing that sound again, I wasn't nervous about spending the flight next to her anymore. It felt like I was back home again.

By the time our complimentary meals arrived three hours later, we had spent the whole time talking about people we'd grown up with and where they'd wound up. Most of them hadn't left Indiana County. Those that hadn't wound up in Philadelphia like me, I'd lost track of after my parents died. My kids kept trying to get me to use Facebook to find my old friends, saying it would help us all reconnect, but I hadn't seen the point.

It turned out that Pamela had an account, but mostly used it to keep up with her nephews and people who had gotten a service dog from her. Maybe if I'd realized that I'd be able to find her, I'd have signed up. But it had seemed like such a hassle at the time. I guess that served me right.

The in-flight meal of a grilled chicken sandwich and ceasar salad was not the best I'd ever had. It was, however more than enough to fill my stomach, and gave me just a little bit more courage to ask her what I really wanted to know - where she had been all this time, and why she'd never reached out.

PAMELA

I couldn't believe how much Martha had changed while still being exactly the same person she had been when we were girls. I wondered if she thought the same of me.

"So, what brings you to Glasgow?" She asked, her

voice bright. "And what does this beautiful lady have in store for her?"

Crouton wagged her tail. She always knew when she was being complimented.

"Crouton, here, is in training to be a service dog for a young Scottish enby with epilepsy. I've done the majority of her training, but she'll need to work directly with her handler to learn their particular needs."

"What does enby mean?" Martha wrinkled her brows.

"It's short for nonbinary, like saying the initials NB," I explained. "It's someone that-"

Her face cleared with understanding and she cut me off with a wave.

"Oh! One of my grandchildren is nonbinary. They're ten and haven't decided what pronouns to use yet," she laughed. "I hadn't heard the word enby before, though."

I smiled, and her gaze softened.

"So you had children after all?" I asked. "You always wanted a whole brood of them."

"I did. Not as many as David and his wife, but enough. Joseph and I had two wonderful children, and we've been blessed with five grandchildren. You?"

I shook my head.

"Nope. Never married or had kids. It wasn't in the cards for me. Instead, I had lots of puppies, supported Ryan and helped Celia raise her three boys."

"Puppies are pretty great," she laughed. "Celia had kids? I thought she was going to travel the world and never settle down."

"Three! She did do the traveling thing for a while, though. It's how she met her husband, Mordecai. He's a very sweet Israeli man. Here, let me show you."

I pulled my phone out of my pocket and opened it to

my family photo album. I had hundreds of pictures of the boys and their families, all saved to the cloud for easy access. That way, no matter where in the world I was, my family was always with me. It made even the worst travel days a whole lot easier. Handing it to her, she scrolled through it with a smile that knocked ten years of worries off of her face.

"They seem lovely," she murmured. "Are they Jewish like their father?"

I nodded.

"Celia converted before they were married. She's been a much happier person since. The boys have never seemed unhappy with it."

She nodded again. A small wrinkle formed between her eyebrows as she scrolled through them.

"Where's Ryan in these? He used to love the camera. Couldn't keep him away from it if we'd tried."

I could feel my face falling even as I tried to smile. Crouton whined and put a paw on my knee, grounding me as much as she could in this unfamiliar environment.

"Ryan passed away about fifteen years ago."

"Oh, Pammy, I'm so sorry to hear that. I know how hard it is to lose a loved one."

I took a deep breath, running my fingers through Crouton's curls. She may not have been my service dog, but she was doing her job anyway. My eyes focused on the pale band of skin on her ring finger and I found the courage to speak again.

"Apparently people with Down's Syndrome are more prone to early onset Alzheimer's than others, and it was all downhill from there."

She reached across Crouton and laid her hand on mine. Warmth spread through me at her touch.

"I'm sorry he's gone. He was a great kid who I'm sure grew up into a great man."

I looked up at her and my breath caught in my throat. She was looking at me with so much love and sympathy in her eyes that I couldn't help but smile, despite the heaviness in my heart.

"He did. He lived a great life, and I was glad to be by his side for it." I sighed and she squeezed my hand. "You would think it would get easier to talk about all these years later."

"I know that feeling well. My Joseph passed away just about a year ago and it's still hard to talk about him."

"Joseph was your husband?"

She closed her eyes and leaned her head against the seat, still facing me.

"He was the best husband I could have asked for. A good man, a good Christian, and a good father." She looked sideways at me and smiled. "And his Scottish accent was to die for."

"You did always love a man with an accent," I laughed. Every time we'd watched a television show as kids, she hung off the words of anyone that had even the most remote traces of a western accent or a British one. I recalled spending most of the time watching her, instead of the show. "What was he like?"

Her smile finally reached her eyes when she opened them a few seconds later. Those hadn't changed at all, though the face around them had grown much older.

"He was silly," she stated. "He was always singing or cracking bad jokes, no matter where we were - in the car, doing yardwork, even in the aisles at the grocery store. The kids were so embarrassed, but I loved it. He knew how to make everyone smile, from the grumpy old ladies to the babies in their strollers."

He sounded wonderful, like exactly who my quiet friend would have needed by her side. Judging by the dreamy look in her eyes as she looked down at our intertwined hands, he must have been a hell of a man. It looked like she'd really loved him. She cleared her throat and looked up at me.

"Your turn to share, Pammy. What have you been up to for the last fifty years?"

I squeezed her hand and smiled.

"That is a long story. You're gonna want to get comfortable if you want to hear about that."

She pulled a bottle of water from the cupholder and took a long drink. She crossed her ankles and shifted so her whole body faced me.

"I'm ready when you are."

PAMELA

I was both drained and electrified by the time our plane started its descent towards the Scottish coast.

Crouton had behaved herself for the most part, though she had been more interested in one of the women sitting in front of us than I would have liked. In the pup's defense, she had smelled distinctly of sugar cookies. Even my mouth had watered a little. I thought I'd trained her not to sniff other people unless she was off duty, but I guess the boredom of the long flight had gotten to her. Even I had to admit that twelve hours was a long time for a dog to sit around doing nothing, even if she had napped.

I had dozed off for a while, too. I couldn't wait to get into a real bed. Martha and I had spent most of the flight talking and laughing. We'd even exchanged phone numbers so we could keep in touch once we landed, which was much better than the last time we'd separated.

Back then, I hadn't realized we were leaving Blairsville forever. At 13, I hadn't really understood how much care Ryan needed that he couldn't get in a town that only had one doctor to go around. That was why we'd moved from our cozy farmhouse to the city apartment that hadn't had a phone. Money didn't go quite as far in Philadelphia as it had in Blairsville, so I'd had no real way to keep in touch with the kids I'd grown up with.

This time, though, I did have a choice. We might have different plans for our time in Scotland - she intended to see the sights for the last time, while I planned to sit down and figure out a new business plan for myself - but I wasn't going to let Martha out of my life again so easily. Not this time.

Once the plane's wheels were firmly on Scottish soil, she helped me get my bag out of the overhead compartment. Being all of 5 feet tall, I had trouble reaching the back where she'd accidentally shoved my luggage. It was a sweet gesture on Martha's part.

It was especially difficult to reach given that I had to keep a hand on Crouton's harness to make sure she didn't find herself whisked away by someone who thought it would be a great time to get a free puppy. It wouldn't have been the first time someone tried, so it was better to be safe than sorry. She had someone just on the other side of the gate that was eagerly awaiting all of the love and assistance she could offer.

Crouton also probably needed to pee, I realized. That would explain some of her antsyness. Lord knows I did, but I was hoping to avoid having to use the airplane bathroom any more than necessary. Someone had vomited all over the room within an hour of takeoff. They had cleaned it, of course, but there was no good way to air out the smell without actually airing the room out. I was looking forward to using a restroom that didn't smell of someone's semi-digested lunch. We just had to make it off this plane.

Martha and I had been separated from each other in the crush of people before I got to the baggage claim, thanks to the slew of large men that were trying to get off the plane just a little bit faster than everyone else. Not that that was likely, given the fact that there were people swarming around us as soon as we hit the terminal floor.

You've got her phone number, I reminded myself. *You will find her again. You will.*

I found a pet area next to the accessible bathroom and I could almost hear her canine sigh of relief as she watered the very fake plants and lapped up what seemed like her body weight in water. A few minutes later, I found an empty stall in the ladies' room and did the human version of the same. Now all I needed was a cup of coffee, and I could pretend to feel like a real human again.

As Crouton and I made our way to the terminal's coffee shop, I kept catching sight of women that looked like Martha. Every time, my heart leapt in my chest like it really was her, but it never was. If she was anything like she had been when we were girls, she would have made her way straight to whomever was picking her up and been on her way home. The airport wasn't anything she would have wanted to explore, but I couldn't help but take it all in while we walked.

When I had a steaming cup of coffee with cream and two sugars in my hand, I was ready to hunt for the family that was to pick me up and take me home with them for the remainder of the week. Crouton and I made our way to the pickup area and scanned the diverse group of unfamiliar Scottish faces, searching for the sign with Thornton on it. Finally, I found a dark-skinned young man holding up a poster board with my name… and Martha's. She stood right next to him, looking as glamorous as she had when she'd first boarded the plane. Somehow, I didn't think I'd be doing as much business work on this trip as I had planned.

MARTHA

I laughed as I watched Pamela realize that we were going to the same place. Joseph's nephew's eyes darted back and forth between us, confusion plain on his face. I didn't explain, though, just shook my head and smiled at her as she cut through the crowd and headed straight for us with an expression that I recognized as a mixture of shock and amusement.

"I take it the universe isn't done having its fun with us yet, eh Martha?"

"It appears not," I laughed.

Of course Pamela and I were going to be staying in the same home. I should have made the connection when she'd said her dog was going to a kid with epilepsy. Joseph's great-nibling, Emilia, was nine and they had been saving for a service dog for a while now. I'd thought there must have been more than one epileptic nonbinary kid in a city with half a million people, though. What were the chances? Apparently better than I thought. Andrew, looking just like his father when he had no clue what was happening, finally spoke up.

"You two know each other, Aunt Martha? Da didn't think you would, even though you were coming in on the same flight." Pamela and I grinned at him before I answered. Her eyes sparkled with mirth.

"We've known each other for longer than your da's been alive, my boy," I informed him. "Now, do you have somewhere to take us or are you gonna make two seventy-year-old women stand in the cold and damp of this airport all night?"

He sputtered out something that probably resembled an answer, but between his accent and his confusion, it didn't even sound like English. Something about it struck my funny bone. I couldn't help but giggle. I tried to hide it behind my hand, but I made the mistake of looking over at Pam. She was doubled over laughing, trying to hide her near-silent cackling in checking on the dog. Andrew waited for us to finish, propping his fists on his hips in a way that was distinctly grandmotherly.

"Okay, okay, you've had your laugh. Now, the car's outside. Do we need to take the dog on a short walk before we head home?"

Crouton, who had apparently been given permission to be off duty, wriggled her entire body in what was clearly pure canine happiness. It was adorable.

"I think that's a yes," Pamela said, a soft smile on her face. "Matter of fact, I'm sure we could all do with a good stretch."

I groaned. I wanted nothing more than to get in the car and get to a real bed. But she wasn't that large of a dog and she'd been on the plane for 12 hours. How much could she pee?

Once again, I was very shortly proved wrong. Despite the fact that it was pitch black outside, Crouton took her time peeing on as many bushes as she could reach while we walked up and down the sidewalk garden outside the airport, even when we could all tell she didn't have a bit of liquid left in her. Finally, we reached the end of the garden, and she wandered around until she found the perfect space to finish her business. Pamela scooped it up and tossed it into the nearby trash can.

"And with that, we are all set," she announced triumphantly. I shook my head. This was why we'd never had a dog when the kids were younger, or even now that they were grown. Too much extra fuss when we were on a schedule. Even if they were very cute. And snuggly.

"Back to the car we go, then," Andrew announced, taking hold of our bags again. "Right this way, ladies."

He had been lucky in getting a parking spot that was near the front door, though that might have had something to do with our midnight arrival and the trains and buses that were waiting for many of the other passengers. I always forgot how predictably *good* public transportation was in Scotland until I came back.

We loaded ourselves into his Volkswagen, cracked the windows so Crouton could smell everything on the roads, and began our trek to the Appleby family home just on the other side of Glasgow.

Not much that I could see had changed since Joseph and I had last visited three years ago other than changing the streetlight bulbs to LEDs. But then, I couldn't see very much at the moment. A Top 40 song by a boy band was playing over the car's speakers while Andrew hummed along. Otherwise, the car and the road around us was quiet.

"Emilia's looking forward to meeting you, Ms. Thornton. She tried to stay up and be up when you got to the house, but she was out before I had to carry her up to bed before I left.

I smiled. Emilia loved to meet new people and she had to be dying to meet Crouton. The nine-year-old had long since gotten too big for her mother or granddad to carry her to her second story bedroom, though I knew that Michael would always try. She was his only grandchild and he had yet to come across anything he wouldn't do for her. He was just like Joseph in that.

"I'm looking forward to meeting her, too, but hopefully it'll be in the morning. I don't want to meet anyone after half a day on a plane," she laughed. "No offense intended."

Andrew chuckled. "None taken. *Nobody's* at their best after that long stuffed in a tin can."

Lord knew that was true. I'd sent my children a selfie from the airport while we were waiting for Pammy. We always did that when we traveled, both to prove we had made it safely and to make the receiver laugh.

Andrea, cheeky as ever, had replied with a comment from her children that "Gramma needed a hairbrush." I had laughed. Kids, especially toddlers, were nothing but honest. And they were right. I did need a hairbrush, but hadn't wanted to dig through my duffel for one in the middle of the airport.

My mother, and Pammy's for that matter, would have been horrified that I'd let anyone see me with my curls mashed from my nap on the plane. However, I had long since decided that it wouldn't be the end of the world if the world saw me at my human default of less than perfect. After all, I was 70 years old. If I couldn't do what I wanted now, then what was the point of being old?

The car had fallen quiet again for the remainder of the short drive through the streets of Hyndland. Their flat was on the top floor of a historic-looking stone building right near the Queensboro Gardens. I had always loved the place.

"Well, ladies, we are home!" Andrew said proudly as he

parked on the street in front of it. "Let's get your bags and head upstairs."

Wearily, we let ourselves out of the car onto the well-lit sidewalk. Despite the many shopfronts around us, the street was quiet aside from the meowing of a few well fed street cats. All of the new cafes and restaurants were dark, but I knew they wouldn't be for long. Morning would come early for the professors and business owners that made up much of the population of this district, and for me.

Andrew led us inside the building, around the front desk and to the elevator door that I had never seen him use.

"What, no stairs tonight?" I teased. He turned, looking at me like I'd grown a second head.

"Did you *want* to go up five flights of stairs with luggage on your back and a dog in hand, Auntie? You're welcome to do so if you'd like. You know where they are. Me, I worked all day and would like to use the elevator I paid for."

That struck my funny bone. I cracked up, my laughter echoing in the empty lobby. I nearly shoved my fist into my mouth in an attempt to stifle it. One of the problems with historical buildings like this one is that they rarely soundproofed as well as they should have. I didn't want whoever lived on the first floor to hear my witch's cackle. That would be a horrible thing to wake up to in the middle of the night.

I caught Pamela's eye and saw she was laughing, too. At least I wasn't losing my mind from tiredness. The elevator dinged and the doors slid open, revealing lush red carpeting and filigreed gold details on the walls. It was a vision of luxury that I hadn't expected from the otherwise work-a-day building. It would make a stunning background for a photograph, but I was too tired to bother pulling out my phone.

We rode all the way to the top floor without interruption and made our way into the apartment with a sigh of relief. Finally, we were home.

———

CHAPTER THREE

MARTHA

I woke the next morning to the distinctly toast-like smell of strongly brewed Scottish breakfast tea and the sound of friendly chatter wafting down the hallway and through my bedroom door. Without opening my eyes, I took a deep breath in through my nose. That smell took me back years, to the days when Joseph would take over and let me sleep in on Saturday mornings. He'd cook a full breakfast for the kids and let them eat it in the living room as a treat. Those were great days. I could almost feel him next to me in the bed.

Just like that, the grief punched me in the throat. Tears welled beneath my eyelids. I knew that if I opened my eyes, I'd be in the same bedroom I'd gone to sleep in. Alone. In Glasgow, Scotland. Not Blairsville, Pennsylvania. Even a year later, I still wasn't used to waking up without him. My therapist told me that someday the loss wouldn't weigh on me so heavily, but it hadn't happened yet. I wasn't entirely sure I wanted it to. I opened my eyes and glanced at the simple alarm clock on the shabby chic nightstand.

I blinked several times before it processed. 10:30 a.m. I needed to get out of bed.

Usually, I was up before seven, even on vacation. Emilia would be bounding in here any moment. Like most children, she had no sense of personal boundaries and limited patience for following her parents' instructions. I would have bet money that the furry addition to the household was the only reason she'd let me sleep this long.

Furry addition.

Crouton.

With a jolt, the prior day's events - and encounters - swept back over me. Pammy was here. My best friend from childhood, who I had thought I'd never see again, was in one of the rooms just down the hall from me. I really needed to get out of bed.

I took a deep breath, wiped the liquid from my eyes and pushed myself up with a groan. I was getting far too old for all-nighters. But, apparently, I wasn't too old to have butterflies in the pit of my stomach. I'd had it on the plane, too. I'd chalked it up to anxiety about the flight, but there wasn't anything to be anxious about now. And it didn't *feel* like anxiety. It felt like... like excitement. That was a weird feeling to have, especially because it was still mixing with the memories and the grief that went along with them. And unfortunately, I didn't have time to deal with them right now.

I had family to spend time with, and I still smelled like plane. I hated the stale sweat smell that always came with traveling, but it was nothing a good shower wouldn't fix. Hot water came with the bonus effect of helping to soothe all the miscellaneous aches and pains that were more normal than I'd like. But then, I was 70 years old. I suppose it was to be expected.

With another groan, I pushed myself out of the bed, keeping my hand near the nightstand just in case. Once I was on my feet, I hobbled over to my suitcase and pulled out my toiletries. It was time to face my Scottish family.

PAMELA

Andrew and his wife, Liliana, were lovely and breakfast was absolutely delicious, but I was still exhausted. I would have killed for a good, strong cup of coffee. Unfortunately, the Appleby's were a tea family. I wished I'd thought of that when I packed my suitcase. I would have packed a bag of grounds with me or ordered some ahead of time. Fortunately, it would be an easy thing to fix with a short walk down to the shops. One of the little shops going up and down the strip had to have something resembling a strong Colombian blend.

Liliana hadn't been awake when we'd arrived last night, but Crouton had already taken a clear liking to her. Crouton had made herself comfortable on the floor between the middle-aged Spanish woman's knees after begging just a little bit for of the mass of food on the table. Liliana had laughed and scratched her on the head instead.

It was good to see that the parents were dog people. Even when they paid my prices, that wasn't always the case. Parents were often willing to do almost anything for their kids, even if they didn't like animals. Emilia hadn't gotten up yet, thanks to her attempt to stay up to greet us the night before. Martha hadn't either, and I was kind of glad for it.

Yesterday's flight had been like a dream, getting to catch up with her like that. I worried that seeing her in the gray light of the Scottish morning would break the spell and things would just be weird between us. I still couldn't believe we were both here, and that we were together again. Even in my wildest dreams, I could never have come up with a meeting like this. It was like something out of a romantic comedy, not like something that would really happen.

Yet, here I was, sipping tea with her in-laws while she slept a few rooms away. We all jumped when Emilia's bedroom door slammed open.

"Da, you were supposeta wake me up when you got hoooome." Emilia yawned accusatorially. "Is morning now! Are they here?"

I smiled, turning around to face the child. She was adorable with dark skin that was nearly a perfect middle ground between her mother's raw umber and her father's deep russet skin, and a crooked-toothed smile that almost literally went from one small ear to the other.

"Hi, Emilia. My name's Pam, and this is-" Emilia cut me off with a delighted squeal and ran to where the dog still sat under the table.

Andrew whipped out his phone and started to take a video with a grin just like his daughter's. We all looked under the table and found Emilia sitting cross-legged about a foot away from Crouton. The pup was watching her with her head tilted and her tongue hanging out.

"You must be Crouton," Emilia said primly. "My name's Emilia. I think we are going to be very good friends."

She held out her hand for Crouton to sniff and giggled

when the poodle clambered to her feet and began licking her face vigorously. Her parents and I started laughing too, the harmony filling every inch of the apartment's open layout.

The creak of another door had us all turning to see who it was, though there was only one person it could be. Sure enough, Martha stepped into the long hallway dressed casually in a chunky knit light blue sweater and a pair of dark linen pants. I guess the previous day wasn't a dream after all.

"Good morning, family!" she called, chipper as ever. I guess some things would never change. I shook my head at the cheer in her voice, catching her attention. "And good morning, Pammy."

She turned the full force of her smile on me and I was glad I was already seated. It was like staring at the sun - capable both of striking you with awe from the joy in it and blinding you if you weren't careful.

"Good morning." I couldn't help but smile back up at her. "Did you sleep well?"

"I did. I had forgotten just how much flying zapped my energy. And you?"

"I slept wonderfully. Not quite as late as you did, though," I said with a laugh. "Crouton woke me up at her usual time for breakfast and a short walk. I have to say, this part of Glasgow is lovely at 5 a.m., even if I would have preferred to not see it."

"Have you ever been here before?" Liliana asked and I jumped. I had forgotten the rest of the Appleby family was still in the room. I shook my head.

"I've spent some time in Britain and Ireland, but this is my first time in Scotland."

"Oh, how exciting!" Liliana exclaimed. "We'll have to

show you all the good spots. If you aren't too busy working with Emilia and Crouton, that is."

"I'd hoped you'd say that." I grinned. Martha was wandering around the kitchen and making herself a plate, picking up a few pieces of sausage to go along with the last of the hard boiled eggs.

"What *is* your itinerary this week, Pam? I've only really got one thing planned for the week, so I'd be happy to show you the sights."

"Well, that's up to your family," I hedged. I had planned to spend much of the trip on my own and didn't want to force her to spend the whole week with me. "I need to teach each of you all of the commands and go over Crouton's diet and what her alerts mean, but other than that, I only really *need* to be here if there's a problem. Unless you'd be more comfortable with me here."

I was babbling like an awkward child, the girl I'd been when I'd moved away from Blairsville, even though I'd explained what I needed to do more than a hundred times over the last 35 years.

"I vote we see how today goes and play it by ear," Andrew said, pulling himself up from under the table with a groan. "I'm getting too old to be sitting on floors. I'm gonna leave that to the professionals today."

I raised an eyebrow at him. "The professional is twice your age, young buck, and I intend to spend my day on your floor. You calling me old?"

"I wouldn't dare." He grinned and bowed from the waist. "My floors are yours for the sitting, my lady."

MARTHA

Once my plate was full of food, I sat down in my usual spot at the foot of the long, rectangular table, looking down the table at my family and enjoying the mid-morning sun peeking through the curtains. Not even a minute later, Emilia poked her head out from under the table, surprising me.

"Aunty Martha! Have you met my new puppy?" I jumped, banging my knees on the underside of the table. That was going to leave a bruise.

"Oh heavens! What on earth are you doing under the table, Emilia?"

"That's where the puppy was." She said this as if it was the most obvious thing in the world. When she hit teenagerdom in a few years, I guessed that it would probably be accompanied by an eye roll and a "Duh." I supposed that she was right. If I'd gotten a new puppy at her age and she was sitting under the table, I wouldn't have thought anything of crawling down there to meet my new friend. Hell, if Joseph had been around, he'd have.

"Well, I guess that makes sense," I laughed. "I got to meet Crouton yesterday on the plane. She's a very good girl."

"Of course she is! All puppies are good puppies! And look at her beautiful face!" She pulled Crouton up so that their faces were level. It was adorable. Instead of responding, I whipped my phone out of my pocket and framed a photo of them. The instant Emilia realized I was taking a photo, she stuck out her tongue. It made almost a perfect mimic of Crouton's happy expression.

"Well, I see two beautiful kids," I laughed, snapping several pictures. "But if you aren't careful, my love, your face might get stuck like that."

"That doesn't really happen, Aunty." She dropped back to her hands and knees and crawled out from under the table and stood beside me. "I'm glad you're here."

"I'm glad I'm here too, sweetie. Now, have you eaten anything yet?" I pressed a kiss to her cheek. She shuffled from foot to foot in a way that told me she hadn't. Her mother didn't miss the meaning, either. She fixed her daughter with a glare.

"Emilia, you know low blood sugar is a seizure trigger for you," she admonished. "Come get a plate and eat so you can take your meds."

"Yes, Mother," she muttered. Again, I sensed a held-back eyeroll and I had to smile. Dutifully, she put together a plate for herself and sat down. She was a good kid, much more responsible than mine had been at her age. But then, they weren't epileptic, so they didn't have to be as grown up as she did.

"Aunty, you're staring," Emilia chided me through a mouthful of potato hash. I stuck my tongue out at her, making her giggle. Even if she had been entirely neurotypical, I still suspected she would have been exactly the same person. Crouton had already realized she was her new person and had made herself comfortable next to her chair. Even as a puppy, she was large enough that her head could easily rest on the seat of the chair beside Emilia's tiny legs. It was the picture of domestic childhood bliss. I really was glad to be here to see it, even knowing that what I needed to do this afternoon was going to be difficult.

Sunny days were known to be few and far between in the Scottish spring. Even though a glance at the weather report said it was supposed to hold out for a few days, I couldn't take it for granted. Today was the day I would spread Joseph's ashes from the top of the Glasgow Tower and say goodbye for the last time. But first, I had to run some errands and prepare myself.

PAMELA

Andrew may have offered his floors to me, but everywhere Emilia and I went in the flat, I was presented with a thick and plush cushion that was so large I could have easily slept on it if I'd wanted to. Emilia and Crouton both had enough energy to make sure that that was not a possibility, no matter how much I might have wished it by the time the early afternoon rolled around.

Child and dog were getting along extremely well. Crouton was even on her best behavior, something I had not expected from the occasionally willful puppy. We had only had to correct her behavior twice in three hours, which was enough to teach the Appleby's how to do so properly. They seemed to be taking it all on board, and I was gratified to see that Andrew was taking notes and videos on his phone. It was a good sign. Their efforts showed me that they were serious about getting the rest of her training right, which meant they weren't wasting my time and energy. That was something I'd always be a fan of.

Martha had left just after breakfast to get all of the things she needed for the rest of her visit here. Blessedly, coffee and creamer were already on the list. After she finished her shopping, she would be going to the Glasgow Tower. The whole family had offered to go with her so she wasn't alone at the tallest building in the country, but she hadn't decided whether she wanted to do it alone yet or not. I hoped she wouldn't go alone. I knew that she had always been strong enough to do anything she set her mind to no matter who was with her, but I could also see that her family loved her enough to want to take care of her. It was lovely.

As if she'd known I was thinking about her, the front door of the apartment opened. Crouton perked her ears and wagged her tail ferociously from where she sat in the center of the living room, and the rest of us turned to see who it was. Martha walked in, preceded by an electric blue rollator with a seat filled with two reusable grocery bags.

Andrew hopped up from the couch and dashed over to her, taking one bag in each hand, then grimacing at the weight. "Did you buy the whole shop, Aunty?"

She stuck her tongue out at him and kept walking with a smile on her face. He stepped out of the way with a laugh, heading into the kitchen to unload her purchases. I pulled myself up from my cushion with a groan as Martha put the rollator out of the way in the living room and joined him, emptying the bags onto the counter quickly and efficiently. Among the fresh fruits, vegetables and snacks that she'd purchased stood a stainless steel French press and a large bag of ground coffee. Thank God.

"You need a boost, Pammy?" Martha asked, holding up a mug without turning behind.

It was like she had read my mind. I could seriously use a cup or three right about now. I glanced back at Crouton and Emilia, seeing that they were both lying on the floor with their arms and legs askew. If they were taking a break, that meant I couldn't finish the last of my training. "Absolutely. Make as much as that thing can hold."

"Eight cups coming right up!" She flipped a switch on the full electric kettle and popped open the bag of grounds. Just the smell alone had my mouth watering. Andrew handed her a cup measure and she poured the grounds into the bottom.

"How's training going? Everybody doing all right?" she asked him.

"So far so good," he told her. "I've been taking tons of notes. And Emilia seems to be learning it pretty well. Hopefully I'll remember everything once the day is done. I'm not sure just how much we have left." He looked to me with one bushy eyebrow raised, turning his last statement into a question.

"You're all doing wonderfully," I reassured him with a smile. "All that's left on my list is for me to work out how to train her to do your particular process for her seizures and then show you how to do it. That's more my work than yours, though."

His brows furrowed as he shared a glance with his wife. "That sounds pretty complicated to come up with a training routine for a process you don't even know. Can you do that today?"

"That's up to you," I told him with a shrug. "I've trained a lot of dogs in my time and I'm used to training people over a day or over a week. If you folks want to take a breather and go with Martha this afternoon, that's fine by me. If you want to power through and get it done, then that's also fine. I'm cool with whatever, as the kids say."

"Why don't we ask Emilia what she thinks?" Liliana asked, stepping up beside her husband and taking his large, callused hand in her much smaller one. "She's just a kid and she's been at this for a while."

"I wanna play!" the child in question piped up. We all laughed. "Crouton needs to sniff all my stuff not spend her whole life training."

"Well, I guess that's our answer." Martha shook her head. "I guess she isn't up for the museum today, which I was expecting. I honestly wasn't expecting any of you to join me for this. I'll be fine on my own."

I could see a wrinkle between her eyebrows that hadn't been there before. That was a wrinkle I recognized. She wasn't being entirely truthful with her family, and judging by their faces, they didn't realize it. I raised both my eyebrows at her and she shook her head again, knowing I'd caught on to her.

The kettle beeped, telling us all that the water was boiling. She pulled it towards her and pulled it off of the heating element to let it come to a decent temperature for the French press. I was glad she seemed to know what she was doing. Many people didn't realize that if the water was boiling when it went in, it would leave the coffee tasting burnt and disgusting. That was such a waste of good coffee, and I didn't want to wait a minute longer than I had to for what my great niece called "speedy bean juice."

She poured the water in and set a timer on the stove. When she turned back towards us, she had a smile on her face, but that wrinkle was still there.

"Pam, I want to show you something. Walk back to my room with me?" Martha's voice was quiet, but clear. I shrugged, gesturing for her to lead the way. Whatever she wanted to say, I guess she wanted it to be between us alone.

We walked down the hallway in silence, our shoulders bumping as we crossed through the slim doorway. I pulled it closed behind me and leaned against it. Martha was silent when she turned to face me.

"Did you know that you still get that wrinkle between your eyebrows when you're lying? It's a little less noticeable now, but I know what to look for." A real smile curled up on one side of her mouth at that.

"I did know that. Joseph loved that wrinkle. And you noticing it… it makes this a little easier." She looked down at me, chewing her bottom lip. That was a new habit to me. "Will you go with me? Um, to the tower."

I blinked. I hadn't expected her to invite me. We barely knew each other now. Sure, we had been inseparable until the age of 13, but it had been 50 years since then.

"Are you sure?" She nodded.

"I'm sure. Everyone else here knew him and they have their own grief to deal with. I just... I want today to be about him. And me, a little. I want... I want it to be a simple goodbye. But I also don't want to be by myself." She cut herself off and glanced at me, as if she knew she had been rambling. It was adorable. I smiled at her.

"Of course I'll go with you," I told her. "Family can be draining, but I didn't want you to have to deal with this by yourself. Besides, I hear the Glasgow Tower is amazing."

She grinned at me and I knew I had made the right choice. I would never get tired of seeing her smile.

MARTHA

Pammy stood beside me, marveling at the building in front of us. She was beautiful, light reflecting off of the stark white tower and onto her pale, wrinkled skin. I found myself wondering what she would have looked like in her prime if she was this stunning now.

When finally I tore my eyes away from her, I realized that the Glasgow Tower really was an architectural masterpiece. It wasn't exactly what you might think of when you think of a tower in Scotland. Usually, that brings elaborate stonework and stained-glass windows to mind. That wasn't at all what this tower looked like. It looked more like something out of Star Trek with the way the tall thin spire rotated naturally in the wind. I was glad it wasn't too windy today. The bottom portion of the building was a science museum and was usually open, even though it swayed with the winds. The viewing deck at the top was only open in optimal conditions, though. It had been a few years since I'd been in it, but Joseph had always been awed by it.

He had done some research into the building because he loved learning how things worked, and had told me once that it was designed to look like the wing of a gigantic airplane had been set into the ground vertically overlooking the river. It could also rotate a full 360 degrees, which made it an interesting building to stand in. I wasn't sure exactly how that worked, but I guess I didn't need to. I just needed to take the lift up to the viewing deck and to do what I came here to do.

"Do you want to see the inside or just stay out here watching it all day?" I teased. She jumped and color rose to her cheeks, as if she had forgotten I was there. I grinned at her. "Come on. The inside's even cooler."

"I'm not sure how it could get cooler than this," she said, but still joined me at the entrance with a smile that made my heart feel lighter instantaneously. With Pam by my side, I was pretty sure that I could do this.

We made our way inside and I purchased two tickets to the museum and lift. Apparently, whoever I had spoken to on the phone had actually made a note that I wanted to spread ashes from the viewing platform, because the girl at the register told me to let them know when I wanted to go up and they would clear the area out for us. That was more kindness than I'd expected from a group of strangers dealing with an old white tourist woman.

Pammy and I walked around, pointing out the activities that would have been the most fun for us had we been younger and fitter. All around us, kids of all ages played with interactive musical machines, surgical operation simulators and physics games. The building swayed slightly beneath our feet and echoed with a cacophony of sound from the machines and children's laughter. It was perfect.

From somewhere in the room, I was sure I heard a theremin. I hadn't seen one of those in a long time, and it had been longer since I played. It probably should have stayed that way. The result was hilarious. The theremin was a difficult instrument to get to sound halfway decent, let alone master, and I was not good enough to do either. We both had better luck making music with the infrared harp, to the delight of several nearby families.

By the time we circled back to the front desk, I finally felt ready to finish this. I had a promise to keep, my very last one to the man I'd spent forty years loving and laughing with, and Pam was going to help me to feel less alone while I did so.

They asked us to wait for a few minutes while they cleared the deck and cranked open the windows. When a group of kids flooded out of the elevator, the girl who had been working the front desk ushered us into the unadorned, and kind of scary, steel box and started us on the way up.

The elevator creaked with each rack it passed on the way up to the 330 foot viewing platform. Pam shifted uncomfortably at the sound, keeping one hand firmly gripped on the handle of my rollator. Her face was ashen, only getting worse the higher we went up. Realization swept through me.

"Are you afraid of heights, Pam?" She didn't move her body at all, simply shifted her gaze to meet mine and gulped.

"Not... exactly? More... small spaces. And falling." She shuddered, dropping her gaze to the floor again. A wave of sympathy washed over me. I couldn't blame her for being scared.

"Would it help if I held your hand?" I asked before I could think about it. Her gaze snapped back to mine in surprise. I held my hand out to her, hoping that the slight shaking of the elevator would cover the way my hand trembled.

With a deep breath, she put her other hand squarely in mine. It was smaller and daintier than mine had ever seemed. She must have gotten a manicure before we left, because her nails were perfectly shaped and painted almost the same color as her burnt sienna hair. I hadn't noticed that before.

In the blink of an eye, the elevator doors opened and we stepped out, hands still clasped tightly. What we saw caused us both to suck in a breath. All around us were rounded glass panels that showed off more sky than I'd ever imagined. The view of the city skyline was absolutely stunning. With the wind racing through my curls and Pam's hand in mine, I felt more alive than I had in nearly a year.

I took another deep breath, squeezed her hand and let go. It was time to let Joseph go. Reaching under the seat of the rollator, I pulled out the vacuum-sealed box with his ashes in it, a pair of scissors and a zippered plastic bag.

"Um, Martha?" Pam asked, blinking at me in what I could only guess was confusion. "What is the plastic bag for?"

"Oh! I'm keeping a little bit of his ashes. I wanted to plant a memory tree with them," I explained. Her face cleared of confusion.

"Oh, right. That's a thing you can do now. Do you need any help?"

Now it was my turn to be surprised. I hadn't expected her to be an active participant in this, to even want to be one, but now that she offered… it would make it a whole lot easier to handle everything with an extra pair of hands.

"You know what? You can hold open this bag for me while I pour." Taking the bag from me, she prepared it and waited for me to get the other bag open. "Ready?"

"Ready," she confirmed. Gently, I tipped the bag so that a slow stream of coarse, light gray ashes flowed from one to the other. It was strange. I'd expected there to be some sort of smell to the ashes, but all I smelled was the river below us and the scents of the city.

Once the zippered bag was nearing fullness, I tilted my bag back up to an upright position and breathed deeply. Pam zipped it up and double checked the seal on it before placing it gently back into the under-chair bin of my rollator. I breathed a sigh of relief and turned to the girl who'd been standing with us.

"Are you ready, ma'am?" She asked respectfully. To my surprise, I was. I kept expecting the grief to come back and punch me in the face, but I just felt determined. Now that I had started, I needed to finish this.

She led me to the one window that had a rail and a half-opening and stood to the side. The box clutched in my hand, I stepped up to the railing and marveled at the view of the city below us.

"Goodbye, Joseph. I'll meet you again someday," I murmured, and opened the box wide so that his ashes could flow out into the air of the city he was born in. After barely a minute, the box was empty. He was really gone. The sound of soft footsteps came up behind me, and Pam wrapped her arms around me, allowing me to lean on her. Finally, I wept.

PAMELA

A sort of quiet peacefulness surrounded Martha and I as we walked along the banks of the River Clyde. One of my hands rested atop the handle of Martha's rollator for balance. I was usually pretty steady on my feet, but we were the only people out here on an uneven riverbank. Martha could lift me, I was sure, but I would much rather not have to worry about falling today. She had enough to deal with without also worrying about me breaking a hip. Besides, it was nice to be so close to her, even if we weren't speaking very much.

The river was beautiful. Some recreational boats sped past us on their way away from the docks, sending a mist of murky water to cool us as we walked. There were signs stating the rules for the water, but we didn't stop to read them. Tourists like us wandered around while local families with young children played on the shore of the river.

Despite how physically and emotionally draining today had been, I wasn't tired. I simply felt content, like this was exactly where I was supposed to be. I couldn't help but wonder if this would have turned out to be a very different trip if I'd had a different seatmate on the plane.

"If it was a little later in the year, this whole section of the river would be full of children enjoying the outdoors," Martha told me, jolting me out of my thoughts. "Joseph told me this used to be the lifeblood of the city. Most of the British navy was built right here for a very long time. It's amazing how time changes places and things, but it can never truly change the way people feel about them."

"Or how people feel about each other," I murmured before I could stop myself. I felt my cheeks go pink, hoping that she hadn't heard me. But of course she had. She was standing less than a foot away from me, her eyes locked on mine with a sense of wonder in them that set my heart racing.

Was it possible that the way I felt about Martha truly hadn't changed since I'd seen her last? Could I still be in love with Martha Rogers Appleby even though the last three days were the first times I'd seen her since I'd moved away from Blairsville? Oh, that might be a problem.

"Pammy?" Her voice was concerned, and when my gaze met hers, her eyes were sharp with focus. "Where'd you go just now?"

"Um," I cleared my throat, hoping to come up with an answer that didn't sound as outlandish as the truth would. I couldn't tell her that I was still in love with her on the day that we spread her husband's ashes over the city. That was crass and insensitive at best. I decided to go with a version of the truth. "I was just thinking that it's amazing how we've reconnected after so long apart."

Her answering smile was soft but brilliant. She placed a hand on mine on the rollator with a gentle squeeze before turning her gaze back to the rolling river. Behind us, I could hear someone playing music through a wireless speaker.

"It almost feels like someone in heaven was pushing us towards each other," she murmured. "Maybe Joseph and Ryan met up there and are having some fun at our expense."

I laughed. I liked the sound of that. It was exactly the kind of thing that Ryan would happily be a part of. As I listened more closely to the rush of the waves, I recognized the song that was playing - Elvis's "I Can't Help Falling in Love with You." I'd know those melodies anywhere. To have it play now... it was almost too perfect.

"Well, we might as well make the most of it, then," I told her, holding out a hand like a gallant gentleman. "Would you care to dance?"

She placed her hand in mine and I placed the other on her hip, scooching the rollator out of the way so that we could sway to the beat of the King's crooning voice. It was a perfect moment.

———

CHAPTER FOUR

PAMELA - 1965

MARTHA AND I WALKED SIDE BY SIDE ON THE GRAVEL ROAD towards town, our bikes creating a barrier against the world around us as we talked about everything and nothing. My parents had left for the weekend to take Ryan to another doctor's appointment.

Ryan's appointments were getting more and more frequent and they were three hours away in Philadelphia. I hated to be in the car for that long just to sit in yet another doctor's office and then spend the night in an uncomfortable hotel. I would much rather have been anywhere else but there.

This time, Martha and I had convinced them to let me stay with her family for the weekend, and it was great. My parents had left some money with us and we'd both been given fifty cents each and permission to spend it however we liked. We just had to be back at home before the streetlights turned on.

We had plans for the day ahead of us and it was going

to be awesome. A new soda shop had opened up last week and they apparently had bubble gum that could make bubbles bigger than your head. We planned to see which one of us could make larger bubbles, and it was going to be the perfect day.

As soon as we turned onto the tarmac of the main road through town, we paused to look at each other. Identical grins spread across our faces as we had the same idea.

"Race you to the store?" I challenged her. Without saying anything, she pulled her blonde curls up into a ponytail that barely kept them contained and fixed me with an intense expression that nearly knocked me over.

"Loser buys ice cream!" she cried, hopping on her bike and pedaling off.

I scrambled to catch up, laughing and hollering all the way. "Cheater!"

I should have expected it. Quiet, she may be, but she never let a competition pass her by if she could win it. And win she did, as I knew she would. I didn't care.

By the time we put our bikes on the rack outside the soda shop, we were both covered in sweat and out of breath, but we were still laughing. We weren't the only kids there. Several of our classmates had their faces pressed to the giant glass windows that showed off a shop that was jam packed with every kind of treat we could imagine.

Martha grabbed my hand and tugged as I stood behind them. My heart skipped a beat when I looked up into her face. She was grinning fit to burst, showing off her adorably crooked teeth.

"Come on, Pammy. You owe me an ice cream!"

In that moment, I would have followed her anywhere just to keep holding her hand. Luckily, I got to keep doing just that. Our hands swung slightly as she led us into the shop. The smell of pure sugar washed over us like we had just walked into pure heaven.

Martha stopped short, and I could see on her face that she was a little overwhelmed. With a squeeze of her hand, I took the lead. It felt like half the town was in there with us, chattering amongst themselves and stuffing their faces with a variety of snacks and fountain drinks. I couldn't remember the last time I'd seen this many people outside of a church service. Winding through them felt like going through a maze, but eventually we made it to the counter.

There were twenty-eight different flavors in buckets behind the counter - everything from fruity flavors like banana and black raspberry to chocolate chip and fudge ripple to fancy flavors like swiss almond and peppermint. My mouth was watering already just looking at them. After a minute, Martha leaned towards me.

"Pammy, I want a cone of fudge ripple."

Personally, I was leaning towards peppermint. There was nothing like ice cold ice cream that left a tingly cool feeling in your mouth when it was so hot outside.

Plus, it was the only flavor that wouldn't taste absolutely terrible with bubble. I had a chance to blow a bubble large enough to contain even her ego at this moment. There was no way on earth I was going to miss out on that.

PAMELA - 2019

I woke up the next morning to an empty bed. It was the first time in... a long time that I'd woken up without a furry creature or three taking up every inch of spare bed. Blinking, I glanced at my phone and realized it was almost

9 a.m. Wow. I must have been more tired than I thought with the jetlag and yesterday's excursion to the top of the tallest tower in Scotland. Raising dogs for the last 30 years had forced me to be more of a morning person than I'd ever wanted to be, and with the time change, I'd expected to wake up much earlier than that.

I lifted my arms above my head and stretched, enjoying the crackle and pop of most of the joints in my back. I had amassed quite a collection of stiff muscles and bones in my 71 years and it was always good to make sure they were all still working. Some people said that popping joints would give you arthritis, but it hadn't happened to me yet, so it probably wouldn't anytime soon. Even if it did, I was old. You were supposed to get arthritis when you were old.

I rolled myself out of bed, eager to get my day started, and got started on my morning routine. I loved my work, and today was the exciting part. I got to learn what Emilia needed from her service dog and make sure that the whole family new how to train Crouton to do what she had to. But first, I needed to get dressed and start brewing the coffee.

I dug around in my suitcase until I found the jeggings my nephews had bought me and a flowy blue cap-sleeved blouse that always made me feel pretty. It was perfect for looking professional and still being comfortable while getting up and down with the dog all day. Now I looked and felt human enough to interact with the Appleby's - and Martha.

By the time I reached the kitchen, the water was already boiling in the kettle. I looked around, trying to see who had started it, but didn't see any of the family members.

"Good morning, sleepyhead!" I jumped. Martha had come up behind me, two mugs in her hands.

"Martha! You nearly scared me to death!" She took in my posture, the shock on my face and my hand clutched to my heart, and raised an eyebrow skeptically before setting the mugs in front of the French press.

"I'll be sure to have 'died of fright before coffee' on your tombstone, then." That made me laugh, which brought her bright smile back to her face. Cheeky woman.

"Where is everybody?"

"Andrew took Emilia and Crouton to a doctor's appointment, and then he's taking Emilia to school. Liliana is in the restroom, I think."

As if on cue, we heard the flushing of the toilet and then the unmistakable sound of someone washing their hands. By the time Liliana reached the kitchen, the water had cooled enough to pour over the grounds. The sweet, nutty smell of brewing coffee filled the room and I breathed it in deeply, already feeling more awake.

"Good morning, Ms. Thornton," Liliana said amiably. "Did you sleep all right?"

"Oh, I slept wonderfully, thank you!"

"I'm glad to hear it. Andrew had to take Emilia to a doctor's appointment and then to school, but he should be back this afternoon with the dog. I hope that doesn't mess up your schedule too much."

"Oh, not at all!" I assured her. "My schedule is your schedule. Besides, as I told you yesterday, I can't do much with Crouton until we talk about what Crouton needs to do to alert you and your husband to a seizure or other health issue with Emilia."

"Well, that's fine then. We don't really need Andrew for that, unless you really want him here. I can walk you through what we need to do." She sat at the kitchen table behind a laptop and what looked to be a cup of tea.

"If that's what you'd like to do, we can start as soon as I get some coffee and some food," I offered.

"That sounds perfect," she agreed. "Please help yourself to anything you like in the kitchen."

We did so, pulling together a few fried eggs a piece and reheating sausage in a frying pan. When the coffee was ready, so was the food. Sitting down at the table, Liliana fixed me with an inquisitive gaze.

"So, I've been doing some research and I've read that trained animals can tell how serious the seizure is? Is that true?"

"Yes and no," I explained. "Crouton is a young dog who's never worked with another handler before, so she'll need to get used to Emilia and her needs. It can take between two weeks and six months before she can really act as a proper service dog, but she will get there. They seem to have an innate sense of how to help their human best."

Liliana looked like she was processing that information, then she typed a quick note on her laptop. I smiled. Andrew would be pleased, if he was as thorough about this as he was the training yesterday.

"Is it possible to…" she paused, and rephrased her question. "We would like the dog to be able to call one of us on her cell phone if there is a minor incident, or call 999 if it's something major. Is that something Crouton would be able to do?"

I nodded. That made sense to me, since she was so young. "With some assistive technology, absolutely. There are programmable buttons that come on bracelets for Emilia to wear or that can be attached to a dog's vest that we could put into use here. You can program them and then train her to press one button in the case of a focal seizure and another for grand mal seizures."

Liliana wrote all of that down, then looked back up at me. "I would like to do that, please. Where should we purchase these devices? And is it possible to start training her with them now?"

"They'll probably need to be purchased online, but I have some fake ones that seem similar to what you'll be sent. That way you can work with Crouton in the meantime and not have any accidental 999 calls."

Her face lit up. "That sounds perfect! And we'll pay you for them, of course."

"Exactly," I grinned. "Unfortunately, the rest of this work will have to be done once Crouton is back. We'll use a lot of the techniques I taught you both yesterday but I want to make sure Crouton listens to you before we leave."

"We?" Liliana looked at me with confusion written in the way her lips were parted and her brow wrinkled. I couldn't tell if she thought I meant leaving with Martha, or leaving with Crouton. Either way, it wasn't accurate.

"Oh, no, sorry. I meant I, not we. I'll be leaving all on my lonesome," I laughed. The younger woman took a sip of her tea before replying.

"Not really. You two are leaving within an hour of each other. It's funny how that works out, doesn't it?" Martha and I exchanged a glance that said it was funny in a weird way. Of all the flights to and from the United States, how had we managed to plan our arrival and departures so neatly? It felt like fate was giving us one more push.

PAMELA

The day had flown by while I worked with Crouton and the Appleby's to help them learn the training process and ensure that everything was going as planned. They would make perfect handlers for the poodle, but by the time dinner rolled around, I was exhausted.

And of course, it was the night that they had planned to stuff us full of every Scottish delicacy they could think of in honor of my first visit to the lovely country. Some of it was homemade - Liliana and Andrew had snuck away a few times to make sure everything was cooking properly - but most of it had been ordered in from a list that was longer than my elbow of restaurants around town. They were making sure I would get the best taste of Scotland possible, despite my protests that they were going to far too much effort over it. I had to admit that it made an impressive spread nonetheless. The kitchen smelled amazing.

Most of the delicacies for dinner involved at least one form of meat. Everything that didn't was mostly made of potatoes and turnips. Emilia happily named each of the dishes that lined the center of the table - haggis, black pudding, neeps and tatties, fish and chips, leek and tattie soup, clapshot soup, hot scotch pie, and potato scones.

I had no idea what half of those were, but she was so happy to tell me about them that I couldn't help but be excited. I'd have to be strategic to try everything, so I planned for three different plates. The first plate I served myself a little bit of the haggis, black pudding and a scoop each of neeps and tatties. Looking at them more closely, I could see that they were mashed turnips and potatoes. They might have been Scottish vegetables, but those at least were familiar.

Haggis wasn't nearly as intimidating as I'd expected it to be. It looked like a mix between ground beef and liver pudding. When I took a bite of it, I realized that that's almost exactly what it was - just with more oats and some different spices mixed in. The mashed turnips were delicious, to my surprise, and made a perfect counterpoint for the black pudding. Mashed potatoes, as always, hit the mark for me.

Next, I decided to change it up with a small bowl each of the two soups. Leek and tattie was leek and potato just like we'd have had at home. Clapshot was like neeps and tatties mixed together with chicken stock, chives and fried onions. I could have eaten that all day on its own, but I had three more dishes to try - potato scones, fish and chips and hot scotch pie. Luckily, I knew a little bit of what each of these would taste like.

If anyone had spoken through the meal, I hadn't heard them. Martha had picked her preferred dishes out of the lineup, as had the rest of the family. I felt their eyes on me while I ate, but I didn't care. I had never been a shy eater, especially when it came to new foods.

On top of the enormous dinner, desserts covered the counters. These were a little more familiar and they looked delicious. Homemade shortbread, something that looked like a trifle but that they called a cranachan, some kind of candy that Andrew was going to deep fry, and a "pudding" that was actually some sort of toffee cake. Unfortunately, I was absolutely stuffed full. I didn't think I could eat another bite.

"Anyone else in need of a break?" I asked, laughing. Everyone at the table groaned in agreement. "How about we heat some water for tea and coffee?"

"That sounds perfect," Liliana agreed. "Andrew, I did all the ordering and cooking today. You and Emilia get to tidy up."

"Aw, Ma! I don't want to clean up!" the kid whined, making Martha and I both smile.

"You read my mind, love." He pressed a sweet kiss to

his wife's cheek. "Em, grab your plate and let's wash up. No whining, my bug."

With a heavy sigh, she did as her father asked and accepted her fate. I held out a hand to Martha. "Let's go deal with the beverages, shall we?"

She took it with that smile that made me feel all wobbly, and together, we made our way into the kitchen.

MARTHA

The next few days flew by. Because of the work that Pam needed to do to train Crouton while Emilia was at school, I hadn't managed to convince her to come out and explore the city with me in the five days we'd been in Scotland. Not yet, anyway. I'd always been able to convince her to do fun things with me when we were younger, and I intended to put it to the test as soon as she finished her video call with her eldest nephew.

Today, Emilia was taking the sweet dog to her third doctor's appointment of the week and getting used to being on her own. Liliana was at the office today, which meant we were left to our own devices. That meant that she had no reason not to come out with me today.

The Pam I knew when we were younger would enjoy George's Square with its variety of historical architecture, the City Chambers, the art museum and up and coming boutique shops. I could only hope, while I waited, that she still enjoyed both art and history.

I pulled out my phone and realized I had a missed call from my son, followed by a text message asking if I was free. That usually meant something was going wrong, but he had followed up with a goofy selfie with him and the kids. It must have been a teacher workday, for all four of them to be home at once. I smiled, noticing that my 10-year-old grandchild in the center of the photo had lost another one of their teeth and was beaming for all they were worth. The 7- and 4-year-old were also grinning. They really were cute children, and I had nothing better to do, so I texted back.

MARTHA 10:47 a.m.

I'm free this morning. Waiting for my friend to be ready to go explore with me.

DEAN 10:48 a.m.

We've got something to share with you. Feel like video chatting us all?

SOMETHING TO SHARE, eh? I didn't bother to reply, simply opened the app and pressed call. Dean apparently wasn't ready for the call, because I heard quite a bit of shuffling but couldn't see anything on the screen.

"Hello? Anyone there?" I teased. The movement intensified, creating almost a static sound. I pulled the phone away from my face with a grimace.

"Hang on, Mom!" Dean laughed. When I could finally see what was happening, the children were all squished onto the sofa with their parents on each side of them.

"Hi, Gramma!" Gabriel's tiny voice rang out. "When are you coming home? I've got some really cool stuff to show you."

"Soon, buddy!" I laughed. He always had stuff to show

me. "I'm gonna come visit you next week with Aunt Andrea."

He pumped a small fist in the air and I laughed again.

"How's your trip, Mom?" Dean asked, ruffling his youngest son's hair and smiling.

"Oh, I'm having a great time! Did Andrea tell you who I met on the plane?" I had spoken to her when we'd gotten home from the Glasgow Tower, since she was up late with her teething toddler.

"She said you met an old friend, but didn't share much more than that. Why?"

"You remember my friend Pam from all the pictures I have of when I was younger? Well, I hadn't seen her since we were 12, but we wound up being assigned the same seat on the plane! And, it turns out that she's the one who's been training Emilia's service dog and she's been staying with the family, too. It's been wonderful spending time with her again." I had to stop myself before I spilled all my guts out to my grandkids. I just couldn't believe how happy I was. I hadn't expected that from this trip.

"Wow, that's amazing!" Lizbeth chimed in from the other end of the sofa. "You sound really happy. I'm glad you're having a good time."

"Me, too," I agreed. "But Dean said you had something to tell me? This sounds important, if it can't wait until I visit next week."

She grinned back at me, then looked at her kids. They nodded seriously, even Gabriel, then burst into smiles when Dean counted down from 3.

"We're having a sibling!" They cried in unison when he reached zero. My jaw dropped. All five of them looked absolutely thrilled, and I was, too. I knew they had wanted another child.

"What? Oh, Lizbeth, that's amazing! Congratulations, you two! When did you find out?"

"We've known for a few months. We wanted to make sure there were no big issues before we told anyone, though." Dean beamed at his wife, then back at the phone screen. "I accidentally let it slip to Andrea yesterday and wanted to make sure you got the news from us, first."

"Oh, of course. I'm just, oh I'm so happy for all of you!" I was starting to get weepy, I realized. And then the grief hit me again. Joseph had so loved all of his grandchildren. He would have been thrilled to learn about another one. I took a deep breath, trying to keep my negative emotions in check.

"Um, we had something we wanted to ask you, though," Lizbeth hedged, rubbing her belly. Dean took over for her.

"We would like to name this baby after Dad, with your permission." My breath whooshed out of me, and there was no stopping the tears now.

"Mom? Mom are you okay?" Dean's voice was frantic. "We won't if you think that would be too hard."

"Don't be ridiculous," I cried. "I was just thinking how much your father would have wanted to meet them. He would be thrilled to have a grandchild named after him. Of course you have my permission."

Now Dean and Lizbeth were crying, too. The kids just looked confused. A voice from just around the corner brought me back to the apartment around me.

"Martha? I thought I heard you crying. Are you all right?" She stuck her head into my room and then drew back when she realized I was on video. "Oh, I'm sorry! I didn't mean to interrupt!

"Oh, no, you weren't interrupting! These are happy tears." I waved her in with one hand and wiped the tears off my face. "I was just chatting with my son and his family. I'm going to be a grandmother again!"

A grin split her face and my heart swelled. "Congratulations, everyone! May everyone be happy and healthy! I'll just, uh, show myself out."

"Actually, we should probably go, too. It's time for these three to do their homework." All three kids groaned. "But we hope you enjoy the rest of your trip, Mom. Get home safe!"

"Send us a selfie!" James chirped just before I ended the call. I laughed. I would take one later while we were out and about.

I got up from my seat on the bed and wandered to Pam's room, where she was tidying.

"So, you have nothing to do today." I reminded her.

"That is true. I assume you plan to change that?" She laughed.

I grinned, showing every one of my teeth. I certainly did.

PAMELA

Her plan, it turned out, was to explore the entire center of Glasgow in one day. I had read about George's Square while I was researching what I wanted to do on this trip, and this was one of the places on the top of my list. I'd spent more time than I wanted to admit watching people on the video camera they had mounted on one of the buildings.

Looking at it now, I was glad that I had made it out here. It had rained earlier this morning, and was calling to do it again in a few hours, so the square was nearly empty.

It was even more beautiful than I could have seen on the webcam, even with the world being slightly damp. Buildings built out of red and grey stone surrounded the square, each serving a different purpose.

Statues were centered in the cross-shaped walkway, with a statue of Sir Walter Scott atop a column that had been mounted on a square base that stood higher than all but one of the historic buildings in the center of the square. The rest of the statues, dedicated to other historically important people like a young Queen Victoria and Robert Burns, had foregone the column and kept closer to the ground. It was stately and beautiful, and I was glad to have seen it in person.

Martha was taking a curious delight in playing tour guide, telling me when the buildings were built and why. It was interesting to see so many buildings that had formerly been hotels but were now guild halls and office buildings. It was like nothing you would have seen back home. The true gem of the square was actually a municipal building. The Glasgow City Chambers wasn't the oldest building there, but it was the most beautiful piece of Victorian architecture I had ever seen. It got better the closer we got because you could see even more of the details, like the carving of Queen Victoria above the entrance and the Statue of Liberty replica in front of the central tower. It seemed like every inch of the exterior was decorated in some way, and on another building it might have been overwhelming, but it was just right for this one.

Even Martha couldn't help but marvel at the art and architecture as we entered the building, even though I knew that she had been here before. Her brow knit in what looked like confusion as we reached the entrance hall and found ourselves blocked by an unmoving group of people.

"Are we behind a tour group?" I asked, frowning.

"I don't think so…" she murmured. "Let's see if we can find a way to sneak around them."

She grabbed my hand and pulled me to one side with a wink. With a little bit of good old American pushing, we finally made our way around the group. Only, what we found on the other side was not a tour guide, but a man on his knees before another gentleman who had his hands clasped over his heart. We couldn't hear what was being said because of the distance, but it was clear what was happening.

"Oh, a proposal!" Martha gasped. "How wonderful!"

The crowd began to cheer when the men wrapped each other in a tight, romantic embrace, not giving a damn that they were surrounded by a bunch of tourists. I looked over at Martha, realizing that she was crying again, though she still had a smile on her face.

"Happy tears, I promise," she laughed. "I love proposals like that. Public, but still intimate."

I shook my head. Of course she would. Martha had always loved showing all of her emotions and sharing them with the world. I shuddered at the thought of something like that happening to me. What if the person wanted to say no? Then they were in public where everyone would judge them. It was not for me, to say the least, but I could see how happy it made others. And, truly, that was the important part, I reminded myself as I held Martha's hand. I was happy just where I was.

MARTHA

By the time we were done exploring, I was starving. I had forgotten just how much there was to George's Square.

Luckily, it wasn't far to the restaurant I had planned for us to eat at. The Urban Bar at the Brasserie had a very odd name, but I'd been told that the quality of the food was unmatched.

I'd wanted to come here the last time Joseph and I had visited, but we hadn't managed it. Built out of a historic building like many of the others overlooking the square, the interior was cozy and sleek. There was a combination of u-shaped black booths with white tablecloths and two-person black tables with green velvet cushions. Each table had a tall, square jar with a tealight in it offering soft, personalized lighting. It was beautiful.

A lovely Indian waitress showed us to our seats and handed us the menus. There wasn't a lot on it, maybe a dozen options, as was the case with fancy restaurants. It all looked delicious, from the parmesan crusted scallops to the bacon and red pepper tart to the 5 spice chicken and the burger.

Pam and I debated which ones we wanted to try until finally, we settled on the confit duck hash for me and the curried salmon for her, with a glass of a white wine we couldn't pronounce.

We kept all of our topics of conversation light, talking about our families and what they had been up to since we been gone but there had been a question on my mind the whole time we'd been in this country. Finally, I couldn't stand not knowing any more.

"Pam, can I ask you something?"

She raised her red eyebrows at me and waved her fork in a gesture that I guessed meant yes. I set my fork down gently and took a deep breath. Keeping my eyes firmly on my plate, I spoke, asking the question that hadn't left my mind since I'd realized who she was on the plane.

"Why didn't you ever tell me that you were moving?

You had to have known. I mean, it's not like they packed everything without you noticing."

"What?" she asked, her mouth still full of the aromatic curried salmon. "What are you talking about?"

"When you left Blairsville? You hadn't talked to me for a week for some reason and I didn't know you were leaving until I showed up at your house that weekend and the movers had cleaned it out."

"Are you kidding me? You'd known for a month that we were moving." I gaped at her, flabbergasted.

"I most certainly did not! You never told me. I know we overheard your parents talk about it, but you never told me for sure." Her face went pale and she set her fork down with a clatter.

"I didn't?" Her voice was barely a whisper now.

"No, you didn't." My voice was quiet but strong. If I had known she was moving, my teenage years, maybe even my entire life would have been completely different. I would have found out where she was living, gone to Philadelphia to see her. "If you had, I wouldn't have let you go without saying goodbye."

"Oh, Martha." Tears were streaming down her face now, bringing her mascara with her. "Oh god. I'm so sorry! What you must have thought of me all these years!"

Now I was weeping into my hash along with her. All this time, it was just a case of the worst miscommunication in the world.

"Why didn't you call me? I didn't know your new phone number. I couldn't have called no matter how much I wanted to."

"I thought you didn't call because... I thought you were still upset with me over giving you the cold shoulder because you thought that that boy from class was cute. I thought... oh Jesus, I was such a fool."

We spent the rest of the meal talking about our dreams and plans for the future. When we made it home, I washed my face and wrapped my curls in a satin wrap, knowing that I would dream of the future we could have had if only we'd communicated a little bit better.

PAMELA

I wasn't sure how I felt as I wandered around the flat collecting all of my things on the last night of my visit. It was rather astonishing just how many of my things had migrated to every other room in the flat, but it gave me time to think, at least. And the Lord knew I had a lot to think about after this week.

I both couldn't wait to get back home and out of the Appleby family's hair and was ridiculously worried about what might happen between Martha and I once we returned to our side of the Atlantic. We had had so much fun together exploring the city chambers and the art museum that it was clear there was still some possibility of a relationship between us.

Dinner, in addition to being delicious, had been illuminating and helped us to hash out a lot of old resentments that had festered in both of our hearts over the years. It was a relief, really. I wasn't sure if she had any sort of romantic feelings toward me the way I still did, but I hoped she did. Even if she didn't, if we just kept in touch, we could have the friendship we'd promised each other so many years before.

That was a good thing. I don't think I would've been able to handle it if we reconnected after all this time and hated who the other person had turned into. My heart would have been just as broken as it had been when my family had moved away all those years ago. Just like back then, I had no idea what the future would hold, but I was a grown woman who got to make her own choices. I was going to make good ones this time.

———————

MARTHA

The cab ride to the airport was a quiet one. Our flights were even later ones this time, leaving at 1 in the morning, so we'd chosen not to force Andrew and Liliana to get up with us. Pam was typing something on her phone and humming along to a slow song on the radio that sounded familiar but that I didn't quite recognize.

I stared out the window, watching the stars fade as the sun rose over the Glasgow skyline and thinking about everything that had happened over the past week.

It had been a rollercoaster, full of literal highs and lows. Now that I'd spread his ashes, I felt at peace with Joseph's loss. I had also had a realization. I still held quite a bit of love for Pam.

He wouldn't have wanted me to spend the rest of my days alone, even if neither of us could have predicted that I would fall in love again almost a year to the day from his passing. I'd been wanting to say something, but it always seemed like the wrong time, or we'd been interrupted, but now might be my last chance.

I had to say something, I realized, and I had to do it before I got on the plane. I wasn't going to risk losing her without saying anything again.

"Pam?" She looked up from her phone with a quizzical expression. "Can I say something?"

"Sure. Give me just a second to finish typing this email." I did so, waiting until she'd put her phone in her lap to start talking. Once I started, I had to finish this. I had to know for sure.

"You know, my mama always worried about my heart, even before you left. At first, I thought it was because she didn't want me to love girls, but it turns out she was mostly worried about everyone in the world I'd fall in love with and allow to break my heart. After you left, I thought maybe she was right. That maybe the joys of falling in love weren't worth the heartache of being alone later, or that it would cause irreparable damage to my already cracked heart.

"But then I met Joseph, and God, you would have loved him. He would have loved you. We were so happy for so long, and we had the best children. But now he's gone and I'm old and my heart is actually failing me the way mama always feared it would. My kids aren't sure they're comfortable with me living on my own. And you're here. You, of all people, were sitting in my seat on the plane."

My chest was heaving and I knew my face was red. I had never felt this vulnerable in my life, and I could only hope that it wouldn't be for nothing. The words had just tumbled out of my mouth, but I wasn't done. I couldn't stop now. I took a deep breath and continued telling her the whole truth of my feelings for the first time.

"Seeing you sitting there, it was like Joseph was standing behind me saying, 'Now's your chance, Martha.' And you know what? I'll take it. You're standing here with me as I let him go. Now's *our* chance. The world's changed enough that no one would bat an eye at us together, and the universe is screaming for us to give love a real shot.

"I have loved you since the day I met you, Pamela Diane Thornton. I have never forgotten that. If you say you don't love me, I'll get on that plane tomorrow and never contact you again. But I think you do love me. I think you've loved me for just as long as I have you, and if that's true, I won't leave the airport till you're back in my arms and we can make a plan for whatever the future may bring."

There. It was out. There was no taking it back now. I felt free, and also a little bit nauseous. Funny how often those two feelings went together no matter how old you got. I held my breath, waiting for her to respond and second guessing every choice I'd made all day. This was the worst place I could have done this. Who confesses their love in the back of the cab? And then her face spread into a smile and the nausea morphed into a tornado of butterflies the way it always had. God, I loved her.

"I love you, too, Martha Rose Appleby," Pam laughed. "I don't know how we're going to merge our lives together, but we can sit down and figure that out at home. For now, you just have to get on the plane. I'll be right behind you. I promise."

Unbuckling my seatbelt, I slid over on the cab's seat and wrapped my arms around her. She pressed her lips to my cheeks, my nose, everywhere she could reach until finally I captured her mouth with mine. With our lips pressed together, it felt like coming home.

I don't know how long we stayed wrapped up in each other, but at some point, the cabbie cleared his throat loud enough to get our attention.

"This is very sweet and all, but we've arrived at the airport, ma'am, and the meter runs until you've exited the vehicle. You should probably, um, go somewhere else."

I blushed, embarrassed but happy. My eyes flitted to meet Pam's and we giggled like schoolgirls as we got out of the cab. While I double-checked to make sure we hadn't left anything behind, she paid him. I hoped she was giving him a hefty tip for having to deal with us. When she was done, she returned to my side, placing her small hand on my lower back.

"Come on. Let's go start the rest of our lives."

CHAPTER FIVE

PAMELA

"WILL PAMELA THORNTON PLEASE REPORT TO THE attendant's station in Terminal 4? Pamela Thornton, please report to the attendant's station in Terminal 4."

My eyes shot open at the words blaring over the speakers in the terminal I'd been napping in. "I didn't miss my flight, did I?"

I wasn't sure how they'd know even if I had. There were probably 400 people seated in the same area. Plus, I'd set an alarm on my phone. I dug through my pockets and pulled it out, only to find a banner on the screen reading "10% battery remaining. Please charge."

Well, shit. That was something I'd need to deal with. But first, I guess I needed to speak to the flight attendants. I couldn't imagine what they needed me for. My flight wasn't supposed to start boarding for another half hour. Creakily, I wound through the rows of seats, dodging outstretched legs and wandering children until I reached the desk.

Two anxious-looking white men in suits and two flight attendants stood behind the glass desk with the airline's logo. That wasn't a good sign.

"Hi, you called me up here? I'm Pam Thornton."

"Ah, yes." One of the men said, straightening his tie. I waited for him to speak again, but it was taking too long.

"Well, can I help you with something?" My clipped tone showed my impatience. He swallowed hard and looked at his companions. One of the flight attendants rolled her eyes and stepped forward.

"Ma'am, I'm sorry, but there's been a bit of a problem. This flight was overbooked and your name was chosen in a random draw as one of the single passengers to give up your seat. We've taken the liberty of rebooking you on our next flight out, which leaves thirty minutes later."

I closed my eyes and counted to five, trying to contain my disappointment and unnecessary rage. This would be fine. I would manage. Martha could wait another half hour for me.

"Okay. Fine. I checked my bag. Will that be transferred to the new flight?"

"Yes, ma'am. We've already taken care of that. Thank you so much for your understanding."

"Thanks for letting me know." I pulled out my phone and typed out a text letting Martha know so that she wouldn't worry. As soon as I hit send, my phone died. And my phone charger was in my checked bag. I wouldn't have access to a charger until I got on the plane and borrowed one from someone else. All I could do was pray that my message had gone through.

PAMELA

Finally, I made it onto the plane. I had one ticket, and no one was sitting in my seat. Even though I'd known Martha wasn't going to be on this flight, I was still disappointed not to see her white curls fall over her face while she looked at something on her phone.

Instead, there were two broad-shouldered white men seated in both the aisle and window seat. I hadn't been lucky enough to avoid the middle seat this flight, even if I had been bumped from my scheduled flight, but I would survive. I just needed to charge my phone.

I took a deep breath after placing my suitcase into the overhead compartment. Martha would only be an hour ahead of me and we were going to meet at the coffee shop near the baggage claim.

We had a plan. If anything went wrong, we had each other's phone numbers. I wasn't going to lose her again. Not this time. However, that plan didn't stop me from being incredibly anxious about what the flight and our futures would hold.

"Ma'am, do you need some assistance with your bag?" I nearly jumped out of my skin at the sound of a voice at my elbow. It was one of the flight attendants. I really needed to start paying more attention when I was standing on an airplane.

"No, thank you," I told them with a sheepish smile. "I've got this."

"Very well, ma'am. Let us know if you need any help." They nodded and continued down the aisle toward the cockpit. It was time for me to sit down and hope the sleeping pill kicked in soon. That would get me through the majority of the flight and let my phone charge now that I was seated. All I could do now was hope that the text had gone through before my phone died.

MARTHA

That had been the worst flight I had experienced in a long time. There had been a crying baby behind me, a smelly, snoring man in the aisle seat, and I'd accidentally packed my headphones in the bag that I couldn't access while we were in flight. I had never been more thrilled to be on solid ground.

Whipping out my phone, I saw a text from Pam that said "Can't wait to see you." That made me smile. I texted my daughter that I had arrived and that she could pick me up at 4:15 when she was done with work. All I needed to do now was find somewhere to sit while I waited for Pam to get here.

MARTHA

I was getting antsy. And hungry. It had been three hours and according to the flight schedule that was constantly updated on the big screen in the airport's cafeteria, Pam's flight was due to come in any minute now. I couldn't wait to see her again. Excited, I grabbed my duffel bag and made my way to the baggage claim, just like we had planned.

I found myself a chair where I could both see the schedule and Pam would be able to find me once she landed and plopped myself in it. Pulling out my phone, I texted her directions to how to find me and sighed.

We had only been separated for half a day this time, but it felt like it had been yet another half century. Being without her was like yet another piece of my heart was missing in a way I hadn't thought was possible for anyone other than Joseph. I couldn't wait to see her again, but waiting was exactly what I must do.

After half an hour, flight number 133581181171 moved from "en route" to "arrived." I waited with bated breath as people began to flood through the doors. My eyes kept scanning the crowd, watching for her bright red hair and lavender sweater.

After nearly half an hour, the stream of people had slowed into a trickle. A few people had gotten my hopes up as I caught a glimpse of colors that could have been her, but she hadn't come through them yet. I was starting to get worried. Even if she'd gone to get coffee like she had when we landed in Glasgow, she would have had to come through here. She would have texted me. I knew she would have.

And yet there was that niggling voice in the back of my head, telling me that maybe she hadn't wanted to see me again, that giving me the wrong flight number would be the perfect way for her to disappear. But I knew her better than that. Or, I hoped I did.

I shot off another text as I tried to push the panic back down my throat. I'd give her another half an hour before I was going to let myself worry. That was the reasonable thing to do. I had to do something in the meantime, though. Otherwise, I worried I would explode from the anxiety. I got up and began to pace, hoping to sweat some of it out without looking like I was a lost old lady. I could make it another thirty minutes.

MARTHA

She wasn't here. She was supposed to be on that flight, but I would have seen her if she'd come down to the baggage claim. I needed to find out if she'd been on the flight and there was only one way to do that - ask for help.

My heart was fluttering in my chest as I made my way to the circular desk near the baggage claim. Two Black men and a Latina woman sat behind the desk tapping away at their keyboards and joking with each other. I hesitated for a moment before I spoke up, feeling ridiculous.

"Excuse me. Um, I need some assistance?" I sounded like a schoolgirl and I hated it, but I wasn't losing her again. Something was wrong. I needed to find out if she was safe. The two men leaned forward.

"Of course, ma'am! What can we help you with?"

"My girlfriend was supposed to be on this flight in from Glasgow. Um, flight number 133581181171?" They were both staring pleasantly, but blankly, at me. I continued. "She didn't come to get her baggage. Can you tell me if she boarded the flight?"

One of the men walked away to deal with someone else, leaving me alone at the counter with the younger, darker skinned of the two men. His stare turned into a frown.

"I'm sorry, ma'am. We're not allowed to give out any sort of flight information. Have you tried calling her?"

Now it was my turn to frown. What did he think I was, a toddler? "Of course I've called her. It goes straight to voicemail every time and she isn't answering her texts either. Can you just tell me if her name is on the flight manifest?"

He thinks for a moment, then shakes his head. The beads in his hair made a musical tinkling sound with the movement. I could feel tears welling behind my eyelids as I took a deep breath and tried to speak again. To my horror, my deep breath turned into a sob as I spoke.

"Please, is there anything you can do to help me?" My voice cracked in an echo of the way my heart was breaking into pieces in my chest. The rest came out in a near whisper. "I can't lose her again. I don't want to spend the rest of my life without her."

The tears began to flood down my face. Even through them, I could see his face change as he realized that she was my romantic girlfriend, not my platonic girlfriend. He reached under the counter and pulled out a travel pack of tissues, then held up a finger. "Give me a minute and let me see what I can do."

I nodded, hoping he could tell the difference between a nod and another of my body wracking sobs. He turned away anyway while I tried to calm myself down. It would be okay. There was some sort of explanation that would make plenty of sense soon.

We knew how to find each other, I reminded myself. It wasn't like before, when we'd had no way to contact each other. We had each other's phone numbers. I knew where she was and I knew she wanted me to find her this time. By the time the young man came back to me with a hopeful smile on his face, I had pulled myself together enough to act like the adult I had been for a long time.

"So, I can't give you any information about the flight manifest or whether your friend was on it, but we can call her over the speakers for you. That way, if she's here, she'll know to come to the desk to find you. And we can keep your number on hand so she can call you if she comes looking."

That almost made me start crying again. That was something for me to hold out hope for. I covered my trembling lips with my hands. "Young man, you have just made my day."

"Well, ma'am, I haven't done anything yet." He smiled shyly at me, pink tinging his apple cheeks. It was adorable. "But I'm happy to do anything to help you find your lady love. Uh, as long as it doesn't get me fired, that is."

Now it was my turn to blush, though I wasn't sure you'd be able to see a difference on my face thanks to the splotches of color from my crying jag. My lily white skin had never been willing to hide any of my emotions from the world, not that I'd ever really tried. I gave him Pam's name and he picked up the phone with practiced ease.

"Pam Thornton, your party is waiting for you at the help desk." His voice echoed in the atrium as he repeated the call three or four times. I gathered my things from the floor and begin my search for a nearby table. I sent one last text to Pam telling her where I was, even though all of the unanswered messages felt like they were whisper-yelling that she didn't want me.

Without anything else to do with myself, I laid my head on my arms and focused on breathing deeply. If I could keep from crying again, I would be all right. Heartbroken, maybe, but all right.

CHAPTER SIX

PAMELA

I TURNED MY PHONE BACK ON AS SOON AS WHEELS HIT THE ground. I had been anxious for the whole last hour of the flight, knowing that the delay would have Martha worrying. If she'd even waited for me at the airport like we'd talked about. I hoped she had.

As soon as airplane mode deactivated, a half dozen texts popped up on the screen, all from Martha in the last three hours.

MARTHA 1:37 pm
I'm back in Philly! See you soon!

MARTHA 1:57 pm
I've set up camp at the baggage claim. Can't wait to see you.

MARTHA 2:26 pm
Are you okay? Please check in. I'm starting to get worried.

MARTHA 2:57 pm

I had them call you over the speakers. I don't know if you heard them, but I hope you did. My daughter will be here to pick me up at 4:15 p.m. I'll be at the help desk until then. I hope you're okay.

MARTHA 3:30 pm

If you didn't want to see me again once we were at home, you should have just said so. This is the worst feeling of deja vu I've ever experienced, and I'm extremely disappointed in you.

Shit. Shit shit shit.

I scrolled up to the message I'd tried to send about the delay before my phone died. A bright red exclamation point flashed on the screen next to it. I very nearly screamed out loud. Martha had no idea my flight had been delayed. She just thought I'd abandoned her here to wait alone. I looked at the time and cursed. It was already 4:27 pm.

Hope and fear coursed through me in equal measures. Maybe she was still there. Maybe I could get to her in time, if I rushed. I just had to get my bag from the conveyor belt and find the help desk. I could do this. If there was any justice in the world, I would get to her before it was too late.

MARTHA

I must've fallen asleep at some point, because I woke with a start at the sound of my phone ringing. Still drowsy, my heart leapt thinking that it was Pam calling me. Then the sound of the ringtone filtered through my brain and it felt like my heart had turned to lead. It was "My Girl" which I used exclusively for calls from my daughter. I slid my finger across the screen and lifted it to my ear in the same movement.

"Hey, Andrea." I tried to put some emotion into my voice, but it came out just sounding tired.

"Mom?" Her voice was anxious. "I've been calling for like twenty minutes. I was about to call airport security to search for you! Are you all right?"

"I'm fine," I said, stifling a yawn. "I fell asleep at a table near the help desk. Are you here already?"

"Already." She snorted derisively. "It's 4:30, Mom. Yes, I'm here. I'm in the pickup parking lot. Do you need me to come in and help with your bags?"

"I'm 70, not an invalid, Andrea." My voice was harsher than it needed to be. I took a deep breath, letting it out through my nose before I spoke again. "I can bring my own bags out, unless you have a particular hankering for airport sandwiches."

"Ooh, actually, coffee sounds really good. They still have a Starbucks in there, right? Could you bring me a latte with two shots of sugar free vanilla?"

I rolled my eyes. "Girl, I am not your butler. If you want coffee, you have to come in and get it for yourself. How about I meet you at the Starbucks and we can walk out together?"

"That sounds perfect, Mom. I'll see you in a few minutes." She hung up the phone and I looked at my still empty lock screen. I didn't even have any Facebook notifications. Pam hadn't texted me. I guess this was it.

I looked over at the help desk, which had a small crowd around it. Hopefully, I scanned them all, hoping to see her small frame. I was disappointed yet again.

With a sigh, I gathered my duffel and purse and made my way to meet my oldest daughter to get coffee before we went home.

———

PAMELA

It took maybe five minutes to get my bag and get to the help desk. When I got there, I was out of breath and my heart felt like it was going to pound right out of my chest. Glancing around wildly, I saw a Latina woman and a Black man behind the desk, with a door open into what looked like a storage room behind them. I didn't see her anywhere nearby. I was too late. My face began to crumple.

"Ma'am? Are you all right?" A tall, light-skinned Black man looked down at me from the other side of the counter with concern on his face. "Henry, get a chair for her. I think she's gonna pass out."

A shorter, darker skinned boy raced out from a back room behind a simple manual wheelchair. He stopped right in front of me, waiting for me to sit down on my own terms.

"No, no…" I waved him off and took another deep breath, trying to get my heart under control. "I'm all right. I just… I'm looking for my girlfriend. She was supposed to meet me here but I'm really late. My international flight got changed and I couldn't tell her and-"

I snapped my mouth shut, realizing that I was absolutely babbling and they probably didn't care. Then I looked up at the young man standing in front of me. He was staring at me with a grin that could only show pure delight.

"Did you just get in from Glasgow? Is your name

Pam?" He asked, the words nearly slurring together in his excitement.

"Yes! Have you seen Martha?" I asked breathily.

"Oh my God, I'm so happy you're here! She was so upset! It broke my little gay heart."

"Is she still here? I didn't see her anywhere."

He groaned. "She literally just walked away like two minutes ago! But she left her number here in case you came. Let me call her for you!"

Before I could protest or say that I had her number, he had already rushed back to his spot behind the counter and dialed the number with a speed that could only be attributed to a lifetime of texting.

The dial tone was loud enough for me to hear across the counter. I stepped up to the desk and waited with bated breath until I heard someone answer on the other end.

Henry didn't even try to keep the grin off of his face as he spoke. "Mrs. Appleby? This is Henry from the Philadelphia Airport help desk. There's someone here who'd like to speak to you."

I couldn't make out the words she said in reply, but I could hear dulcet tones through the receiver. I would know that voice anywhere. He held out the phone to me and I felt like I might faint with relief. Maybe I did need that wheelchair after all.

"She'd like to talk to you." I took the wired handset with trembling hands and held it up to my ear.

"Pammy? Pam, is that you? Are you all right? I was so worried!" Her voice sounded frantic. "Why didn't you call?"

I laughed out loud and the tears I'd been holding in began to descend down my cheeks. "Darling, I'm so sorry I'm late. I didn't mean… I got bumped from my flight but my phone was dead. Are you still in the airport? I can't wait to see you."

"We were just about to leave! My daughter and I are at the Starbucks near the entrance. Meet us here? I can't get back through security."

"Of course, I'll be there as soon as I can." There was no question about it. I'd follow her anywhere in the world. Hopefully, she'd rather have me by her side than two steps behind like I was tonight.

"Hurry, dear. I miss you." The phone beeped three times. For the first time since I'd turned it back on, I finally felt like I could take a full breath. I wasn't too late. We still had a chance to have a happy ending. I just had to act like the heroine in the last act of a romantic comedy and run for it.

MARTHA

I stood there with my phone in my hand, frozen with a beaming grin on my face. This was like a dream come true after a sleepless night. I didn't even move when I felt Andrea's hand touch my shoulder.

"Mom? You okay?" She handed my coffee and looked at me quizzically. The warmth against my fingers pulled me out of the air and back into my body. "Who was that?"

"I can honestly say that I have never been better," I confessed. "You remember how I told you that my childhood friend was staying with us in Scotland?"

"I remember? Was that her on the phone?" She was still confused. I had to make this clearer for her.

"It was! We had such a wonderful time and fell back in love with each other. And she's here!"

I had to laugh at her reaction. Her eyes were nearly bulging out of their sockets, and her jaw would have hit the floor if it could have. I was pretty sure that no one had ever seen her with such a shocked expression on her face.

To be fair, a week ago, I would have had the same expression on my face if someone had told me this would happen. I had never expected to fall in love again. Yet, here I was. Standing in an airport Starbucks with my heart in my throat, waiting for the woman I'd loved for my whole life.

"Is that why you told me to pick you up now instead of when your flight actually came in? Mom, people can change a lot in fifty years. You know that! You barely know who she is now! Are you sure about this?" Her shock was tinged with skepticism now, but I didn't care.

"I know people change, dear, and I intend to spend the rest of my life getting to know every... Oh - there she is!" She'd come around the corner at a near run. Just seeing her filled my heart with joy.

I pushed my coffee into Andrea's hand and dropped my bag to the floor, running towards her as quickly as my legs, and the people milling about, would allow it. Andrea's voice followed me as I ran, calling out "Mom!" I ignored her. Pam caught sight of me and her face was like the moon coming from behind the clouds after a day of rain.

She gripped her bag tightly and made a beeline to where I was. We collided in a tangle of limbs and tears. Her chin nestled into my bosom and mine found its home on top of her head. My arms were wrapped around her waist and hers around my neck. We were enveloped in the floral scent of her perfume and the stale air of the airport. We clutched each other tightly for what felt like both an eternity and the blink of an eye.

In that moment, I didn't care that we were making a

scene in the middle of the airport. The only thing that mattered was that Pam and I were together. I never wanted this moment to end.

"I'm so glad you waited," Pam breathed, wiping the tears from her face "I never want to lose you again."

She rose to stand on her tip toes and glanced at my lips, waiting for permission. I inclined my face and pressed my lips to hers. Just like before, kissing her was like being struck by lightning in the best way. When we broke apart, we were both breathing heavily I stared at her in wonder. I had no idea that kissing her would feel that way, but I never wanted to live a life where I didn't feel that regularly.

She released me from her embrace and took a step back. Using her bag to support her, she lowered herself to one knee on the floor. I gasped, sure that she wasn't about to do what I thought she was.

I stared at her with my mouth agape while people held up their phones around us. Of course this was being recorded.

"Martha, I don't have a plan. I don't have a ring. Hell, I don't even know how we're gonna make this work, but what I do know is this," Her voice started small and clear and grew louder and more confident with every word while I stood there, awestruck. "Every time that I see you, I remember that even on the worst days, there's a possibility for joy. When you're with me, I look forward to whatever the world has to throw at me. We lost so much time out there. Let's not waste another minute. Will you marry me?"

"Are you serious?" I asked, covering my mouth with hands that shook. Pam hadn't taken her eyes off of me.

"As serious as I've ever been about anything," she assured me. I could see the truth of that in her eyes before mine filled with tears at the realization that the first woman

I'd ever fallen in love with was proposing to me. And I could only answer with one word.

"Yes!" I nearly shouted it, then lowered my voice to a more reasonable volume. "Yes, yes yes!"

The airport erupted in cheers and whistles around us as I helped her to get to both feet and crushed her into a heated kiss that told her just how much I meant it.

———

EPILOGUE

PAMELA

I couldn't believe we had made it. The Fiji sand was comfortably warm between my toes. The corded lace of my ankle length gown felt like cooling water against my skin and the hibiscus flowers in my bouquet smelled divine. Everything was perfect. As soon as the music started, I would start walking in front of all of the people Martha and I loved best to go marry the woman I'd been in love with since before I knew what love was. I couldn't wait.

We'd decided that we were going to walk in from opposite directions and meet at the altar instead of one of us going down the aisle. We had started our lives together as equals and we intended to do so while we took the next step on our journey. Not to mention, we both wanted to show off our stunning gowns.

Of course, I hadn't seen Martha's yet. It was bad luck to see the bride before the wedding, and we weren't taking any chances with luck today of all days. But I knew that she had impeccable taste and would look perfect in anything she picked out.

In the six months since we'd returned to Philadelphia, I had never regretted asking her to marry me. In fact, I'd fallen even more in love with her every day since. We'd only waited this long to get married to assure our families that we hadn't lost our minds. The soft notes of the piano arrangement of the Glasgow Love Theme from *Love Actually* began to play. It was time.

Taking a deep breath, I timed my steps carefully to the melody as I made my way toward the altar. There was no one in front of us scattering rose petals or attending our gowns and that was just fine, because there should never be anyone between us now.

When I looked up, the sight of Martha took my breath away. She was a vision in an ivory dress that flared out from her waist and cut off just below her knees, with a beaded lace neckline and headband keeping her white curls out of her beautiful eyes.

I couldn't believe I was really marrying this woman. It was even more perfect than I'd imagined, and she was looking at me as if she felt the same way. By the time we reached the altar, we were both crying and laughing at the same time. The officiant handed us tissues and we dabbed at our faces, trying to avoid smearing our makeup before the ceremony truly began.

"Dearly beloved and honored guests, we are gathered here today to join Pamela Diane Thornton and Martha Rose Rodgers Appleby in the union of marriage," he began, his deep voice easily reaching the back row of the small group of guests. "This union is not one to be entered into lightly. No other ties are more tender, no other vows more sacred than those you will take today. Do any of you who are gathered here today object to these two women taking these vows?"

Our loved ones, a small group that included only our families, stayed resolutely silent until the officiant smiled and nodded.

"If no one objects, then I would like to invite everyone to join us in song in honor of our brides." Martha and I beamed at each other as they began to sing.

MARTHA

I had barely been able to keep it together when Pam walked down the aisle toward me in an almost entirely sheer corded lace gown, with hibiscus flowers whose petals were almost the exact shade of her hair. She was gorgeous.

I felt a shiver run up my spine when we clasped our hands at the altar and knew that I was doing the right thing. I wanted to feel this way every day for the rest of my life. Luckily, she was standing at the altar looking at me like I put the stars in the sky, so I had a pretty good chance that wasn't going to happen.

"Are we ready, ladies?" He asked us. We both nodded and he turned his attention back to our audience.

"It's common for newlyweds to choose to plant a tree or create something at their wedding that will last a lifetime," the officiant informed them. "To begin their ceremony Pam and Martha have chosen to make their planting even more special. They have chosen to plant a tulip tree in an urn that holds some of Martha's late husband's ashes. Martha, if you will."

I stepped forward, still holding Pam's hand.

"Those of you who knew me as a young woman would

have met my husband Joseph. He was my friend and my love for a very long time, and I will never forget him." I cleared my throat, holding back tears for what felt like the billionth time today. "In our vows, we promised to grow old together. Now, he passed away before his time, but he doesn't get to get out of that promise so easily."

The audience laughed, and I waited for them to quiet before I continued. "Pam and I would like to honor him by planting this tree together in his memory, so that we can both keep that promise we made."

The officiant handed me the urn and Pam the sapling. While we planted it, trying very hard not to get the soil on either of our ivory gowns, the officiant read an old Irish blessing that seemed perfect for this moment.

"May the road rise to meet you, and may the wind be always at your back. May the sun shine warm upon your face and the rains fall soft upon your fields. Until we meet again, may God hold you in the palm of his hand."

I would have guessed that not a single eye on that beach was dry by the time he finished. Mine certainly weren't. The officiant handed me more tissues and I wiped at my eyes again.

"Now that we have honored those who came before us, it's time to look to the future. Do you, Pam, promise to share your life and dreams with Martha?"

"I do." Her voice caught in her throat, and I beamed at her.

"Do you promise to support her through good times and bad?"

"I do." Her voice was just a little bit stronger.

"Do you promise to respect, love and stay loyal to her for the remainder of your days?"

"I do." This time, her voice was clear and sonorous, ringing out across the beach. He asked me the same questions and I'm sure I responded appropriately but the world blurred together with joyous tears. The next thing I knew, the rings were in our hands.

"Now, both of you repeat after me," the officiant instructed. "With this ring, I thee wed."

We did so, gently pushing the simple gold wedding bands onto each other's fingers while the crowd cheered.

"Now that you have exchanged rings to be a constant physical reminder of the love you share, you may kiss your wife for the first time."

He didn't have to tell us twice. The crowd around us cheered and hollered as I lifted Pam off of her feet slightly, kissing her for all she was worth - and she was worth a hell of a lot. When I finally set her down, the officiant beamed at us.

A traditional processional song began to play, and I gripped Pam's hand tightly as we made our way down the aisle toward the reception hall together. We were married and all was right in the world.

LEARNING CURVES EXCERPT

Fluorescent lights bounced off of the whitewashed cinder block walls in the hallway of the Bryan Building. It seemed excessively bright compared to the matte gray that stretched across Greensboro's skyline as it did on most October mornings, and Elena found herself squinting a little.

Her head was full of thoughts of the business law class she'd just left, and she was operating mostly on autopilot when an unfamiliar voice said her name.

"Hey, Elena, right?"

Elena turned, taking care not to knock her large bag into the other people in the hallway. She found a short, slim woman at her elbow looking at her nervously. The other woman was familiar, but Elena wasn't quite sure where she knew her from.

As she stared at the woman wearing a long-sleeved flannel shirt-dress while other graduate students flowed around them in the hallway, something clicked in Elena's head — this was one of the girls from her business law class.

"Yeah. You're Cora, right?" Elena mentally crossed her fingers, hoping that was her name. Seeing her nod, Elena continued. "What's up?"

"I've noticed you always do really well on the quizzes and stuff. How good are your notes?" She ran a hand through her blonde hair, nearly shaved on the sides, but with a small pompadour of tight curls on the top, pink tingeing her freckled cheeks. She was the kind of girl who Elena would have guessed to be queer on first glance, between the flannel and undercut.

"Pretty good, why?"

"I, um, kind of hyperfocused on James singing to himself in the back of class today and couldn't keep up with class at the same time. Is there any way you could email me your notes? Or I could copy them from you, or-"

Elena cut her off with a short wave. Cora's entire face was bright red now. There was no reason to make her suffer any more embarrassment, especially in a crowded college hallway full of their classmates.

"I take all my notes on my laptop. I can email them to you. What's your email address?"

Cora's face lit up, showing off her slightly crooked teeth. Elena couldn't keep a matching one from spreading across her own face. Cora handed over a folded sheet of notebook paper with her email address written on it in clear block letters, which Elena folded and tucked into the large purse she carried.

"I'll send them to you when I get to lunch in a few minutes. James is a terrible singer, and I don't think he knows." Elena rolled her eyes in commiseration. James was one of her fellow law students, and she had purposely sat as far away from him as possible in the thirty person classroom. "All of our other professors have banned him from singing in class, but I guess Doctor Burgess hasn't noticed yet or just doesn't care."

"Ugh," she moaned. "It's the worst. I wish I hadn't sat next to him, even if that seat did have the best light. Priorities, right?"

Cora widened her eyes and grimaced in an expression that Elena found strangely adorable.

"I'm ADHD and even with meds, stuff like that can really screw me on a bad day," Cora continued. She rubbed her fingers through the short-cropped hair in front of her ear. Her expression turned rueful.

"That's probably more than you needed to know about the girl begging for your notes. I'll let you get to lunch. I know they keep you law kids on a really tight schedule. Thank you again for the notes, Elena. I really appreciate it."

"It's not a problem. We all have bad days," Elena said reassuringly. "You should have an email from me within the hour."

"Thank you thank you thank you!" She began to walk away, then turned and waved goodbye. Elena's heart skipped a beat.

Walking across the campus to the dining hall, Elena found herself wondering why she hadn't ever talked to the girl before. She was the kind of girl whose aesthetic Elena loved, and she seemed really nice. Then she remembered — she didn't really talk to anybody in the class, except when required. Cora hadn't been wrong about the law students being incredibly busy, and most of Elena's classmates were problematic at best.

Business law was one of the hardest classes to get into at the university they attended. It was a required class for both business and law graduate students at the University of North Carolina at Greensboro. There were never enough sections of it offered for the number of students who had to take it. There were barely enough seats in the classroom for everyone who needed to be in it.

However, it was also one of the only classes that didn't have group projects, which was a relief. Group projects were only helpful if you were a slacker because you could figure out who usually did the work. Elena was usually that person and thus hated group work.

Elena slid into one of the cafeteria chairs that had been designed for much slimmer people than she was. Settling in, she pulled out her laptop and closed the extraneous programs to get to her email.

With a flash of brilliance as she checked her notes for spelling errors, she remembered that there was a free seat on the far side of her self-assigned desk in the classroom. Elena smoothed down the Puerto Rican flag sticker that covered the area next to her laptop's trackpad. Smiling, she typed out an email, attaching the notes.

To: Cora (cemclaughlin@uncg.edu);
From: Elena (emmendez@uncg.edu);
Subject: Bus Law Notes
Hey, Cora,
This is Elena from Business Law with the notes you asked for. Hope these are helpful for you. Let me know if there's any shorthand in here that doesn't make sense, and I'll try and translate it to you.
I remembered as I sat down that there's a free seat next to me by the door, from when that greasy kid dropped out of the program. James is always noisy, so if you wanted to start sitting there, I wouldn't mind. I'd love to get to know you better.
Sincerely,
Elena

Gnawing her lower lip, Elena stared at the email for a few moments, wondering if the last sentence was too forward. Shaking her head at herself, she hit send. Cora would want to be friends or not - Elena being too forward in an email wouldn't change anything but how long it took them to figure it out. She wondered if being forward was even a thing people worried about anymore.

Elena took a deep breath in through her nose and remembered how hungry she was. Dining hall food was no comparison to the homemade food she'd grown up making and eating, but it would do for a working lunch. Elena slid her laptop back into her bag and made her way towards the food, her heart thumping slightly at the idea of making a new friend.

By the time the next class rolled around, Elena had almost forgotten that she'd told Cora about the empty seat. The much shorter girl had already set up her laptop in the seat directly between Elena's usual seat and the wall. And... there was a clear plastic cup of iced coffee sitting on Elena's desk?

"Is someone sitting there?" Elena asked quietly, blinking several times in rapid succession.

"Oh, hey!" Cora jumped a little in her seat, her cheeks coloring a little in clear embarrassment.

"No, no one's sitting there. Um, that's for you? I used to work as a barista and noticed that you bring mocha frappucinos to class a lot, so I wanted to thank you."

"Oh!" Elena made a sound of surprise and set her bag on the ground. "I didn't realize you'd been watching me so carefully. I didn't have a chance to get coffee this morning, so this is perfect! Thanks so much!"

"You're welcome. Your color-coded notes were the only reason I know most of the stuff that's gonna be on the test this week." Cora's cheeks turned an even deeper pink, making her freckles stand out. "I'm hoping that sitting over here will be a game changer for me. I've been struggling with James' singing under his breath all semester and I didn't realize this seat had opened up."

"I think the kid who sat here dropped out entirely last week? I don't even know his name. Either way, I promise there won't be any singing," Elena laughed lightly. "Dr. Burgess also teaches a couple of my other classes, and my notes are probably the only reasons I've passed them all so far. She's a hardass, but she's a great teacher."

"She seems like it. I'm in the MBA program, so the law aspect is less critical for me to know offhand, but it's really interesting, as weird as that sounds."

"That doesn't sound weird at all!" Elena smiled back, glad to know that someone other than her found joy in different aspects of the law. "The law is really intricate and specific, which is why I love it."

She looked like she wanted to say more, but Dr. Burgess swept in and slammed the door of the classroom. The professor threw her purse on the desk at the front of the classroom, and Elena and Cora exchanged wide-eyed glances.

The entire class sat up just a little bit straighter, and aside from the noises of breathing and shuffling, was absolutely silent.

"Hello, class." Dr. Burgess huffed. "Take out a pen and some paper. Pop quiz time."

The class groaned in unison before moving to take out something to write with and on. Elena wondered what had bit her to get her in such a mood today.

Cora had been typing furiously on her laptop, and

Elena felt her phone buzz in her blazer pocket. While pulling out her notebook and setting herself up for the quiz, Elena checked her phone and saw an email.

To: Elena
From: Cora
I like your flag sticker. Want to get lunch later?
Here's my number.
(336) 555-5555

Elena glanced sideways at Cora. She guessed she hadn't been too forward last week. Catching Cora's eye, she nodded, and the other girl's entire face lit up. Elena's heart skipped a beat again, and she couldn't help but smile back.

ACKNOWLEDGMENTS

To X, Chay and Lina for being my cheerleaders and helping me to make this book be the best it could have been.

To Great British Menu and Great British Bake Off, which was my background noise for 90 percent of the writing process. But also, please stop flavoring your food with douglas fir. That shit's nasty.

ACKNOWLEDGMENT

ABOUT THE AUTHOR

 Ceillie Simkiss is a queer and neurodivergent author and freelance writer based in southern Virginia. She has bylines in the Danville Register & Bee, VIDA Magazine, Culturess and Global Comment. She blogs regularly on her website, CandidCeillie.com and is the owner and editor of LetsFoxAboutIt.com.

She loves nothing more than curling up in bed with a book and her many furry creatures, but playing silly video games is a close second, even though she's terrible at them. She also writes as Candace Harper.

It is easiest to reach her on Twitter or via email! She would love to hear from you!

facebook.com/ceilliesimkissauthor

twitter.com/candidceillie

instagram.com/candidceillie

goodreads.com/ceilliesimkiss

bookbub.com/profile/ceillie-simkiss

ALSO BY CEILLIE SIMKISS

LEARNING CURVES SERIES:

Learning Curves (#1)

The Ghosts of Halloween (#1.5)

Wrapped Up In You (#2)

ELISADE UNIVERSE

An Unexpected Invitation (#0.5)

A Knight to Remember (#1)

CPSIA information can be obtained
at www.ICGtesting.com
Printed in the USA
LVHW020354301221
707526LV00010B/734